Donald Trump's Top Secret Concession Speech

as told by

John Sheirer

ISBN: 978-0-692-84537-0

This is a work of satirical fiction based on the established public record of facts. Facts still exist even if Trump and his supporters pretend they don't. Because we're speaking Trump's language, we could call this book, "alternative nonfiction." Bigly.

An audio version of this book is available on Audible.com.

Empty Suit Publications
Sub-Basement, T-Rump Tower
New York, New York

Contents

Introduction

The world seems to have gone insane with the election of Donald Trump to the Presidency of the United States. It's almost as if we are now living in an upside-down world where the South won the Civil War or the Axis Powers won World War II.

I'm reminded of the old *Star Trek* episode where Captain Kirk struggles to make it back to the real Enterprise after a transporter malfunction sends him to an alternate universe where we can tell the Federation is evil because Spock has a goatee. Spoiler alert: Kirk makes it back. I hope we do soon as well.

But what if ...

What if, for a very brief period of time, Donald Trump had actually developed a sliver of moral decency just before the election? What if he thought he was going to lose the election? Even more importantly, what if he thought that he *should* lose the election because he realized that he's a terrible person with no business being president?

What if Donald Trump spent a few days with an audio recorder making notes for the concession speech he thought he would have to deliver on election night?

What if those notes were made public? What would Donald Trump sound like if he had something resembling a conscience?

Read on and find out ...

* * * * *

My name is Bartholomew Tyringham. Please call me Bart. Don't feel bad if you haven't heard of me. Most people haven't. I'm a very minor writer with a decent career of publications. There are thousands of high quality but unknown writers out there in the world. I definitely fit the "unknown" category. The "high quality" part isn't mine to judge.

One person who definitely hasn't heard of me is Donald Trump, and I'd be happy to keep it that way. I'm probably the least likely person on the planet to possess a secret that could change the way we understand the current part-time occupant of our nation's White House.

But, fortunately or unfortunately, one very important person has heard of me. A young woman who identified herself as "Maria" contacted me in late November of 2016. Maria said that she followed my political page on Facebook, "Bart's Banter," and had read some of my relatively obscure blog posts about politics and current events. She was one of the few.

Maria informed me in her initial message that she was a maid who works in the Trump Tower as an employee very close to Donald Trump's closely guarded inner circle. That seemed a dubious claim, but I gave her the benefit of the doubt. She said that she turned to me when she made an astonishing discovery not long after the presidential election.

Once she told me what she had found, I immediately traveled to New York and met with her in an out-of-the way coffee shop in Manhattan. Maria was an attractive young woman who spoke with a strange Spanish accent that didn't seem authentic. She wore large, reflective sunglasses and a long, dark wig with strands of blonde hair feathering out at the edges. Her face seemed vaguely familiar at first. Soon I would realize why.

Maria claimed that she had discovered a digital voice recorder jammed between some cushions of one of the many enormous couches in one of the many opulent rooms that Trump inhabits in the New York building bearing his name. She told me that she had no idea who owned the recorder or how it came to be in the couch, so she decided to listen to a few minutes to see if she could identify the owner and return it. What she heard when she pressed play was the voice of Donald Trump himself.

After just a few minutes, Maria realized that the recording was Trump making audio notes for himself as he prepared for a speech. But this wasn't any ordinary speech for one of his mindless rallies where he ranted about immigrants and rigged systems and "Crooked Hillary" while dishonestly bragging about his own dubious accomplishments.

This was Trump's concession speech.

Maria told me that she took the recorder home to her small apartment and huddled on her own small couch to listen to the entire recording, unable to eat or sleep, both fascinated and horrified by what she had found. She provided me with a sheaf of printed materials that she claimed was a transcript of the entire set of Trump's recordings. She hadn't trusted anyone else with her discovery, so she had painstakingly done the transcription herself (which might account for a few random typos that I left undisturbed in the final version of this book).

She then played several extensive excerpts of the recordings for me, and I was able to verify that this was, indeed, the unmistakable voice and verbal style of Donald Trump. This was not an Alec Baldwin type comedic impression. This was the man himself. I also matched the spoken words from these excerpts with the corresponding locations in the transcript, and Maria assured me that the entire transcript was a direct match to the entire recording.

With Maria's permission, I immediately made multiple copies of the transcript and mailed them to several people I trust with instructions for my friends to hide the sealed envelopes and only give them to me in person. These were secret words spoken before the election by a powerful person with a reputation for attacking political enemies. I wasn't going to risk the transcript falling into unfriendly hands and making its way back to Trump himself.

Maria urged me to publish these transcripts so that the world could have a better view into the mind of the controversial man who was about to become "leader of the free world," as insane as that prospect seems to people who actually understand the awesome responsibility of the presidency.

Maria said that she had know Trump "all her life," which seemed unlikely given her youth and relatively minor position in the Trump household.

Maria also told me that she had even contacted the FBI's New York office to discuss her discovery. After many attempts, she finally got through to a mid-level functionary. When she described the audio files in her possession, the agent only laughed and told her that no one would be interested in the files. If she came across any damning information about Hillary Clinton, on the other hand, she was told to call him immediately.

Interestingly, the young woman I met bore a striking resemblance to Donald Trump's youngest daughter, Tiffany, behind her wig and sunglasses. This could have been merely a coincidence, but I would later discover that the transcripts themselves would provide a clue about her true identity.

Tiffany Trump is Donald's daughter with his second wife, Marla Maples. Maples, unlike Trump's first wife Ivana, doesn't have a legal gag order against revealing the details of her relationship with Trump, and she is suspected to be the source of Trump's partial tax documents sent to the *New York Times*.

Tiffany famously rejected a kiss from her father on national television after the second presidential debate, the one immediately following release of the disgusting "pussy grabbing" tape. Trump himself once said that he was only proud of Tiffany "to a lesser extent" than he was of his other adult children. What kind of father says something like that any time, let alone to the media while running for president? We can only guess at the family dynamics at work in that relationship.

After our New York meeting, I was unsuccessful in subsequent attempts to contact Maria. The profile she used to contact me on Facebook has been deleted, and my investigations into Trump's employees have been futile. It's as if "Maria" never existed. I was also unable to contact

Tiffany Trump through the layers of protection surrounding every member of the Trump family and inner circle, and she has kept a notably low profile since the election, just as she did during her father's ugly campaign.

The preceding background shows how this book came to be. Presented here are the actual words of the actual man who won the election and is now, unfortunately, our president. We seem to have fallen into an nightmare where the least qualified and most corrupt candidate in history has conned just barely enough people to squeak out a dubious Electoral College win and assume office.

These transcripts confirm the biggest surprise in American political history: *Donald Trump himself knows that he's a fraud.*

What follows are the words of a terrible person as he briefly wrestles with the newly emergent knowledge that he is, indeed, a terrible person. These recorded rants reveal a profane mind at times frayed beyond coherence. Now and then, however, he shows a lucidity not seen during his irrational campaign. At some moments, he appears sane, remorseful, apologetic, even sad about

—
14

the damage he had already done to the nation before the election. At times, in rare instances that defy everything we know about him, he seems almost human.

Trump's actions since the election have confirmed what a dreadful person he is. Barring impeachment or resignation, our nation is doomed to at least four years of this wholly incompetent pretender. But for the limited moments of self-reflection provided by these transcripts, we have the small comfort to see that even he might have some kind of a conscience beneath his malevolent exterior.

When his job approval ratings inevitably drop to historic lows and he is faced once again with the knowledge that he's not the person he pretends to be, perhaps that conscience might resurface. Perhaps he might go away at long last and free this country from his greedy grip. In the words of Shakespeare's Hamlet, "'tis a consummation devoutly to be wished."

We all know Trump's thirst for revenge and giddy lust for threatening lawsuits while compelling his rabid supporters to attack anyone who doesn't bow down before him. So I'll call this book a work of "fiction." I'll say that I fabricated these words and the entire story of their origin as a way to deal with my own anger and grief at the election of such a mind-numbingly inappropriate choice to lead the nation that I love. I'll say that I wrote all this frantically in the few weeks between the election and the inauguration. I'll say that I made up the whole thing to mitigate the misery that Trump's con artistry has inflicted on everyone I know and love.

You, the reader, can decide for yourself what's true and what's not. In his dark heart, tragically, Trump himself knows the truth.

Audio File Transcript #1

(harsh clicking and electronic feedback sounds)

How the fuck does this thing work? I press the red button? I can barely reach the red fucking button. American-made piece of shit.

Just another useless nothing that Tiffany gave me for my birthday a few years ago. She said I love the sound of my own voice more than my own children. As bad as her mother Marla, that one.

I guess I may as well get some use out of the stupid thing. The recorder, not Tiffany. She'll always be useless.

Okay, it's working. So, this is Donald J. Trump. Today is November something, 2016. I've lost track. The election is next week, I think. I know I'm going to get my ass kicked and then have to give a goddamned concession speech, so I'm just going to talk into this tape recorder for a while to get my thoughts organized and then turn this piece of shit over to the speech writers.

How do I start this speech? I brag about having the best words, but I'm just a shit-filled gasbag. What the hell, I'll just copy the start of every other fucking speech in history. "My fellow Americans." If Melania can plagiarize, then so can I.

My fellow Americans, the nation has spoken. I lost, fair and square. Yeah, the nation has spoken. As if this country full of idiots could form a coherent sentence. Forty-something percent of this nation might actually vote for me, so this is one stupid-ass country.

Nothing was rigged, okay? If any idiots start mouthing off about millions of people voting illegally, tell 'em to shut their lying pie holes. That was just more bullshit to rile up the deplorables even more. Those assholes will believe anything I say. I may be a compulsive liar, but these dopes are definitely compulsive believers.

But now it's time to talk to the millions of good people in this country instead. It's time to talk to all the ones who voted against my sorry ass. Maybe the deplorables will finally learn something too. Doubtful, but fuck it.

(long pause)

My fellow Americans, I've been forced to do some soul searching. I haven't found one yet, but I'll keep looking because I've got nothing better to do.

My fellow Americans, I'm sorry. I'm so fucking sorry.

(audible sobbing)

Audio File Transcript #2

My fucking staff took away my fucking Twitter.

(sniffling)

Just like that. At first I was pissed off at the fuck heads. I fucking love Twitter. It's perfect for someone with my short attention span. Some people think that I take hours to write each tweet, editing and revising complex ideas into 140 characters. What horse shit. I write each one in about ten seconds.

I just went back and reread some of my tweets for the first time. You know, the ones I really wrote. Not the ones from my staff. You can always tell the ones my staff writes. They sound so fucking reasonable and nice and presidential. Those are the ones where shit is spelled correctly and there are no all-caps or exclamation marks.

The tweets I actually write ... well ... What the hell was I thinking, and what took them so long to take my Twitter away from me? Jesus, it's about fucking time. Weren't they reading the crazy shit I was posting? I used to think that my tweets showed the world how cool and smart I am. Yeah. That's bullshit. Non-stop insults and recycled white supremacist trash made me look a lot more like an asshole than like someone cool or smart. I'm so fucking thin-skinned you can see my internal organs.

My alt-right titty-face supporters like to call liberals "snowflakes" because they think liberals are wimpy. Do they even read my Twitter bullshit? I crave constant approval. I've got no core values of beliefs. I can't stand criticism. I blame everyone except myself. I claim I'm being persecuted. I won't accept difficult truths. Shit. Behold, assholes of the world. I'm the fucking Snowflake King!

Can you imagine if I actually won the election and kept sending out shit like that on Twitter? How fucking presidential that would be. Once this election is over, I think I'll do the right thing and dump my Twitter account. Maybe I'll take up painting like George W. Bullshit did. Why the hell not? I'll paint my little dinky floating in the bubble bath like he did.

Without my Twitter, I had some time to think about what I've done to this country during my campaign. I got onto this internet thingy for the first time and Goobled myself instead of tweeting insults all hours of the night. I think that computers have complicated lives very greatly. The whole age of computer has made it where nobody knows exactly what is going on. We have speed, we have a lot of other things, but I'm not sure we have the kind of security we need. Jesus, that's deep. But, what the fuck, right?

So I Goobled myself, like I said, and I can tell you, folks, I didn't like what I saw. I learned that people record what I say so that other people can watch it and hear it later. Why did no one tell me this? I knew they did that on reality TV, but you would think real life was different from reality TV. I guess not. Shit.

When I looked at myself during this campaign, I saw that I've been appealing to hate and fear and jealousy and bigotry and sexism and a bunch of other -isms that I don't even know the name of. Aww, fuck, I'm sorry for that.

Did you know the KKK endorsed me? How could anyone with any sense vote for me after that? The K-fucking-K-K. The lynching and cross-burning assholes. The rotten-teeth, inbred, knuckle-walkers named Billy-Bob and Jethro and April May June. People with nicknames like "Uncle Myself" and "Cousin

Wife." People who think Mountain Dew is a basic food group. Those fuckers want me to be president. Jesus, I'd vote against myself even if that was the only thing I knew about the whole goddamned election.

The KKK actually endorsed me in their official newspaper. Can you fucking believe that? Who knew those KKK assholes had a newspaper? Hell, who knew they could read? If the KKK wants me, I should just jump off of the top floor of Donald J. Trump Tower right now. Except the Klan-holes would blame "Killary" and still vote for my dead corpse out of low-IQ stubbornness.

I'm just as bad as the Klan sometimes. Did you know I said that we should kill the families of suspected terrorists? Somebody told me that shit is actually an awful war crime. I'm sorry for pimping war crimes like some kind of monster. Why did I think people would vote for me if I acted like a monster?

I said that women should be punished for abortions, as if I have any right to tell them what to do. I'm sorry. When a woman makes a difficult choice about her own pregnancy, that's none of my fucking business. Punishment? What the hell was I thinking?

Just listening to my screeching voice on television should be punishment enough.

I said I'd get rid of gay marriage. I don't even know if I believe that, or if I was just saying it to get the homophobic morons to vote for me. Why would I want homophobic morons to vote for me? Are there even that many homophobic morons left in this country? Anyway, I'm sorry for appealing to homophobic morons.

I even looked at my own website. Who wrote that garbage? Why am I trying to give rich people like me another tax break when there are hungry children in the country? Why do I claim that I'll be strong against terrorism when I'm so fucking terrified that I want to hide the whole country behind a wall? Brave people build roads, houses, schools, hospitals. Fucking cowards build walls.

Okay, do you know they have fact checkers on the internet? Why didn't anyone tell me that I was lying so much? I was mostly just making up crap and repeating the crap my advisers told me to repeat and expecting everyone to believe me. Why would anyone believe all that crap and vote for me? The country can't be full of fucking crap eaters, can it?

I said that thousands of Muslims in Jersey City cheered the attacks on 9-11. Even I knew I was lying when I said that one, but I was hoping it would be a little lie that would take attention away from all my big lies. A few people called me out on it, but most of my supporters just went ahead and believed it.

Are there even a thousand Muslims in Jersey City, New Jersey? I doubt it. But, after a while, I just realized that most of my fucking idiot supporters would believe anything. If I had said that a million Muslims on Mars cheered when Ronald Reagan died, these morons who show up at my rallies would have believed it and would have claimed Obama was the head Martian Muslim. Which is worse? The idiots for believing my lies or me for telling my lies?

Hell, I even lied about not having the sniffles at the debates. Jesus, I sounded like an infant with a cocaine habit trying to snort up the podium all night, but I went on *Fox and Friends* and told those brain-dead couch potatoes that I wasn't sniffling. I blamed the goddamned microphone. What the fuck kind of person lies about sniffling on national television?

Fuck. I'm going to hell.

Audio File Transcript #3

You know who made me shake my head in fucking disgust every day of this campaign? Not Hillary. Not Obama. My idiot supporters, that's who.

Did you hear that some egghead said he analyzed my speeches and determined that I talk to my supporters at a fourth-grade level? It's a good thing, too, because my supporters think like children. Actually, that's probably giving them too much credit. My speeches are like an angry toddler yelling at confused infants. I just toss some alphabet blocks in a blender, barf it up, and they swallow that swirly shit like formula.

They keep saying, "Trump speaks his mind." Yeah, I definitely speak my goddamned mind. That's the goddamned problem. Do these fuckers actually listen to me? They thought I was joking when I said that I could shoot somebody and my poll numbers would go up. Don't they realize that I was talking about how stupid they are? I'm pretty stupid myself, but these geniuses think they can't go swimming when it rains because they'll get fucking wet.

Some day I'm really going to speak my mind and translate my rally speeches into a few sentences, something like this: "All crime in America is committed by immigrants, Obama, and Clinton. Only I can protect you. Bow down before me, helpless white victims. Vote for me or die a violent death. I am your God, you peasants. Most of what I'm saying isn't fucking close to being fucking true."

Dumb fuckers would still vote for me.

"Trump isn't 'politically correct.'" Jesus, I can't believe how many people bought my "politically correct" bullshit. What the fuck does "politically correct" actually mean, anyway? Doesn't it just mean, "Don't say racist shit all the time"? What the fuck do I care about being racist? Money is green. That's the only color that matters to me. But I sure as hell would rather have Jews counting my money than Blacks. Is that racist? Probably. But I don't care.

I've been saying and doing racist shit for years, and nobody seems to care, except sometimes the nigg--

Wait. I didn't say that word. People keep telling me to stop saying nigg-- stop saying that word. I'm trying really hard to stop saying that word. It's just tough to break a lifetime habit, okay? Not using the N-word is almost as hard as not saying cun-- not saying the C-word. But, to be fucking honest, I don't really give a shit.

Just a couple of years ago, I tweeted that Obama was such a bad president that we'd never see another black president in generations. Of course, I would never say that Bush was such a bad president that we'd never see another white president in generations. Nobody would think that made any fucking sense.

But racists loved that tweet because they could claim it was just a general observation without being racist. It was a way of saying if one N-word was bad, then we can just assume all N-words are bad. Here's the best part: I said it without even having to use the N-word. Magically, that makes it not racist in the racist mind.

I'm glad that none of those tapes of me using the real N-word actually got released. But, shit, how much evidence do people need? I was sued and fined for not renting apartments to black people back in the '70s. That's fucking illegal racism. I'm a fucking "illegal" more than any Mexican is. If Hillary had done that kind of illegal racism, Bill never would have been elected just from the stink of being married to her. My racist moron supporters? They don't give a fuck.

The klanners and white supremacists love me. Have you ever noticed that white supremacists are the least supreme white people around? I talked about my superior "bloodlines" a few times years ago, and now they think I'm their fucking new Mein Führer. I know all of my anti-immigrant, anti-Muslim, anti-Obama talk helps racists feel like their views are okay. I help them climb out from under their rocks and step into the sunshine with their racist ideas. And I'm fucking okay with that. A racist vote counts just as much as everyone else's. More, even, because those racists fuckers sure do love to get out and vote.

There are a lot more racist morons in this country than I thought. My fucking rallies are full of these turds. They yell, "White power!" at my rallies, and people slap 'em on the back and hug 'em. If anybody yells, "Black lives matter!" they get the shit kicked out of 'em. So, yeah, being against "political correctness" just means letting the biggest assholes also be the loudest assholes.

I heard the other day that some Republicans are trying to sell my campaign by telling people that I may be an asshole now, but I'll "mature" once I'm elected president. Really? When was the last time a rich, spoiled, arrogant, clueless, 70-year-old asshole has "matured"? I am what I am, dumbasses. Get used to it.

Hey, have you heard this one? "We need a businessman in the White House." Really? Have you dumb fuckers heard of George W. Bush and Herbert Hoover? We tried businessmen in the White House, and the results were fucking depressing. Literally.

And my businesses aren't really something to boast about, although I boast about them every chance I get. No one else will, so I have to. I actually bragged about using my bankruptcies to make money, usually by screwing everyone else. Do these dumbasses not realize that every time I fuck up a business, they foot the bill? Don't they know that every time I make money, it's at their fucking expense? There's only so much wealth in the world. If I'm hogging it up, then farmers in Pennsylvania and construction workers in Florida and housewives in Michigan sure as shit aren't getting any of it from me.

What do they think of when I brag about making money from my fucking bankruptcies? Do they even know that I could have earned more from my inheritance if I had just invested in the stock market and slept all fucking day instead of running my fucking dumbass businesses?

My supporters seem to forget that the business of government is people, not fucking profit. Even I know that, and I'm a borderline sociopath. There's only three people I want to help: me, myself, and I.

My supporters claim that I'll bring jobs back to America. Which fucking jobs are they talking about? Making Trump Ties in China and Trump Suits in Mexico? Can they really be that confused about how I've made my money? I even said in a debate that wages were too high. Weren't they listening? Why the fuck would they want to vote for someone who doesn't give a shit about their lives as long as I can make myself richer?

Hey, do you like my fake slogan, "Buy American, Hire American"? Yeah, guess what, motherfuckers? I buy Chinese steel for my buildings and beg for visa waivers to hire foreign workers for my resorts and hotels. How can people take me seriously? Are they fucking retarded? Oh, sorry. Sarah Palin says nobody is allowed to say retarded, except maybe Rush Limbaugh. Maybe she'll give me a special Papal Palin dispensation so I can say it too. Jesus, she the biggest retard in the whole country, you know, if you consider Alaska part of this fucking country.

Of course, I can recognize that lots of people are having a hard time in the job market. I keep lying about the unemployment rate, but the truth is that it's way down since Obama started cleaning up Bush's shitpile. But lots of manufacturing and fossil fuel jobs are shutting down because of technology and global competition. I don't know shit about economics, but even I know those jobs aren't coming back.

What am I supposed to do, tell a coal miner that he should get a job installing fucking solar panels? I'd lose millions of votes if I came anywhere near to telling that level of truth. But guess what? If I say I can bring those coal jobs back with voodoo and magic tricks, there might be just enough idiot voters in Pennsylvania who'll believe my bullshit. Desperate people will believe all kinds of desperate bullshit.

And think about coal jobs for a second. There are some people who actually believe me when I say I'll keep coal miners working. I know the Kock Brothers have funded lots of global warming denial, but come on people! Anyone who believes me when I say that global warming is a Chinese hoax actually deserves me as their fairyland president. Here's the kicker: These people in coal country hate Hillary even though she has a great program to help coal miners who lose their jobs. I give 'em nothing but promises emptier than Rand Paul's silly head, but they still love me and think Hillary is the fucking devil.

Jesus, really I should be ashamed of myself for taking advantage of those poor fuckers. How long have I been telling people, "You're fired!"? How many times do I have to say that stupid catch-phrase before people get a clue that I'm much happier taking jobs than creating them. You're fired! You're fired! You're fired! You're fired! You're fired! You're fired! You're fired! You're fired! You're fired! You're fired! You're fired! You're fucking fired!

Holy shit! That one shouldn't be all that hard to figure out. If it increases my personal wealth, then, sure, I'll create a job or two here and there. But most of the time, firing people means I don't have to pay them. You do the fucking math. And I'm sure as shit not creating a job by paying you to do that math, just in case you geniuses haven't figured that out yet.

You know who brings back jobs to America? Democrats do. I've been around a long time, and it just seems that the economy does better under Democrats than Republicans.

Look at fucking Hillbilly Bill Clinton. Jobs coming out his cracker ass. And Obama? The average voter is too dumb to know that he's been creating jobs faster than Melania falls asleep on our "very special Friday nights." The dopes who think he's a Socialist don't even know that he's more than replaced all the jobs that George WXYZ Bush dumped down the toilet.

Fucking Obama could walk up to these lily-white assholes and hand them a thousand dollars, keys to a new car, and the down-payment on a house, and they'd piss themselves, call him a commie Kenyan Muslim, and run for their fucking gun collection in their fucking panic room.

These putzes seem to think when I talk about cutting wages, I'm talking about someone else, maybe the guy down the street from them who they don't like, especially if that guy's black or Hispanic. I don't even need to con them with a bait and switch. They do it to themselves.

When I talk about cutting taxes, they think I'm talking about cutting *their fucking taxes*. Fuuuuuuuucking idiots! They think they're on the verge of becoming rich based on some fantasy they developed, probably watching my moronic TV show. One little lucky break, and the cash will just shit on their heads from asses in the fucking sky.

Yeah, bullshit. That's not how it works. Unless their daddies were as rich as mine, that is. These idiots don't realize that their taxes will *go up* if I get my way. And any benefits from the government that they get would fucking disappear. The only people getting more benefits and lower taxes in Trump world are my rich buddies. I am a fucking Republican after all. Everybody who isn't rich will fight over the scraps and watch Monday Night Football on a TV that they can't afford to pay off.

My supporters even think that I'll somehow fix political corruption. Yeah, right. Don't they know that I've been involved in more than four thousand fucking lawsuits? What kind of son of a bitch spends that much time getting sued and suing? A corrupt son of a bitch, that's who.

I keep saying I'll "drain the swamp." Drain the swamp? No, you foolish assholes. I'm the King of the Fucking Swamp! The only way to drain the swamp for real would be to stick a spigot up the asshole of the Republican Party and turn that fucker on full blast.

You'd think if people were pissed off about rich bastards buying politicians, they wouldn't be tripping over their tits and dicks to vote for a rich bastard like me. Maybe they just want to skip the middle-man. They just want me to screw them directly as I fatten my bank accounts at their expense rather than getting screwed by the politicians on my payroll. These people would just offer their fucking keys to a car thief and then wonder why they need a ride home.

Have these deplorables even heard of Trump University? Can they even read? Hell, New York state court ruled that I operated Trump University without a license, and there are three more major lawsuits. Those suckers would have been better off going to their local community college. I scammed millions of dollars from thousands of people just by putting my name in big gold letters on that shiny piece of shit. I'll be lucky to settle those cases for less than $100 million and keep my ass from bunking with Bernie Madoff.

My supporters just go on and on with their shitty reasons to support me. And I have to keep this shit-eating grin on my face as they go on and on while they're thinking, *Hey, this shit tastes good!* That's the sad part. They think their shit tastes good. The pathetic part is that sometimes I get to thinking all that shit tastes good too.

I'm working with Kellyanne on a formula for saying things so my shit-eating supporters will understand. When I lie, Kellyanne wants me to call it "alternative truth." Here's a few of my favorite new ones based on that formula: Donald J. Trump doesn't push for radical policies. His policies are "alternative reasonable." Donald J. Trump has "alternative nice hair." Donald J. Trump speaks with "alternative eloquence." Donald J. Trump is "alternative smart." Donald J. Trump doesn't have small hands. Donald J. Trump has "alternative big hands." Damn, these "alternative geniuses" will believe anything!

When you have to use fake news and alternative facts to win, you're a loser.

"Trump will stop ISIS!" these losers say. They actually believe my rants that I have a secret plan to defeat ISIS but won't reveal it until I'm elected. Holy shit, that's stupid! They think it's okay that I keep my secret plan a secret while thousands of people die from Fucking ISIS? Even I'm not that fucking nuts. If I had a fucking secret pan to stop ISIS, I'd tell it to someone who could go out and, you know, *stop fucking ISIS!* And then I'd take the credit, of course. It would be nice to take the credit for something I actually did myself for a change instead of stealing everyone else's credit like I usually do.

"Trump is self-funded," they say. Nope. Are they so blind that they can't see that I solicit donations, just like every other hack politician. What do these geniuses think the "donate" button on my campaign website does? Do they think it's like one of those "Bill Gates will give you $5,000 if you forward this email" buttons? Do they think I'm a Nigerian Prince who needs them to cash my inheritance?

And I've been funneling my campaign money right back to my own companies as much as possible this whole time. Did people miss it when I was hawking my shit like some kind of carnie at one of my press conferences? Trump steaks, Trump water, Trump vodka. I might as well be on QVC instead of CNN. Fox News has become my own personal marketing company, and those toxic morons don't even know it.

Trump steaks went out of business years ago, but I flopped some dead meat on the table anyway. Nobody fucking cared. My whole fucking career has turned into branding myself, and this campaign is just an extension of that. I'm just a silly entertainer pretending to run for president but really just flogging my stupid brand. I might as well be Captain Fucking Obvious. Who knew all these assholes would take me seriously?

Hell, my campaign rents hotels and meeting rooms from me, buys shit-tons of food from me, and I even pay my corporate staffers with campaign donations. I'll be damned if I'm not going to take the money these idiots send me. Idiot money spends just as easily as smart money. It's all fucking green, no matter how dumb the people who send it might be.

Can you imagine what I'd do if I got elected? How much money could I make running my businesses from the White House? Sure, I could pretend to have my idiot kids run my businesses, but no one would be dumb enough to believe that's the same thing as a blind trust. Wait. They're dumb enough to vote for me, so they'd probably be dumb enough to believe that I'd behave ethically and not try to ride that gravy train straight up Pennsylvania Avenue.

"Trump will take care of our veterans." Don't they know that I stiffed veterans' organizations on charitable donations until reporters shamed me over it?

"Trump won't hide things like those evil Clintons." I won't even release my tax returns, something everybody else does. I've got more shit hidden than a whole season of *Hoarders*.

"Trump puts America first." I violated the fucking Cuban embargo and had dealings with a bank that supports terrorists in Iran. I put my money first, every fucking time, obviously. And even I know that "America First" is a goddamned anti-Jew slogan, but those Breitbart assholes insisted I throw it out there like pig slop for the Neo-Nazis. Are there really that many Neo-Nazi votes out there? The Breitbart boys seem to think so.

"Trump will surround himself with great advisers." Yeah, two fucking words: Breitbart and Bannon. My fucking campaign staff and surrogates are an embarrassment. They are loyal, though, and I value that, at least, even if they are fucking scumbags. If they're not lying through their teeth to protect me, then they're on the phone to Russia all damned day kissing Putin's ass for me. That shit's called loyalty, fuckers.

"Trump will dump Obamacare." My big-mouthed supporters know even less about Obamacare than I do. None of my advisers will even explain to me the difference between Obamacare and the Affordable Care Act. Hell, nobody seems to understand that mystery.

And with no coherent plan from those lazy-ass Republicans in Congress to take Obamacare's place, twenty million people will lose coverage and the insurance companies will go back to fucking over sick people. Not that I care so much if sick people get fucked over. I've fucked over plenty of sick people in my day, some even in my own family. But you can't just completely fuck people over by yanking Obamacare and expecting that no one will notice how fucked over they're getting. People can't be *that fucking stupid* ... can they?

Besides, once they dumped Obamacare, they'd call whatever came next "Trumpcare." And when that fucked everyone over, who the fuck do you think they'd blame?

"Trump will reverse Obama's terrible policies." The policies that cut unemployment and the federal budget deficit in half? Fuck, it's like these people can't read or count.

"Trump will make other countries fear us." They're already laughing at America just for considering voting for me. Even I know that.

"Trump will save us from Muslims who hate America." Like Ghazala, Khizr, and Humayun Khan? Yeah, I learned their fucking names. They *are* what America stands for. God, what a dumbass move I made criticizing these people. Who knew they'd fucking fight back?

"Trump will build a wall and close our open borders." I actually looked this one up on the internet yesterday. Illegal immigration is

down under Obama. Look it up! I was
shocked too! Why the fuck am I ranting
about borders and Mexicans when illegal
immigration is down?

I love to tell stories about the illegals who
rape and kill people because that gets
everybody riled up. But here's something
else I found out: Regular, everyday
Americans commit way more crimes at a
way higher rate than illegals do. You're more
likely to be murdered by Joe Blow down the
street than José Blosé from Mexico. My
fucking wall will just keep Americans from
escaping all the other Americans who want
to Second Amendment them to death. But,
hey, getting people to hate someone with an
accent and a slightly browner shade of skin
is a great way to get votes from all the
pussies out there who are afraid of anyone
dark in the dark.

Fuck, even I know what would stop illegal
immigration. All they have to do is dump
some CEOs in jail for hiring illegals. A few
rich assholes like me getting locked up would
shut down that shit pronto.

That wall? Jesus Christ, have people never
heard of tunnels? Do they think walls can
stop airplanes and helicopters? Did my

supporters skip the fucking grade in school where they taught about the oceans on the east and west and gulf on the south borders? Of all the idiotic things I've talked about in my lifetime, that wall must be the dumbest. And Mexico will pay for it? Yeah, and the moon is made of green fucking cheese.

"Trump's a winner!" they keep saying. Did they watch the debates? I got mass-murdered so bad that Republicans in Congress said they would send their "thoughts and prayers." It was all I could do to keep from crying in front of the whole world.

People told me I didn't do enough "debate preparation." No shit, Sherlock! Hillary fucked me up so bad in those first two debates that I needed a crate of Preparation-H to get ready for the last one.

Shit. I think I'm going to cry right now just thinking about those fucking debates.

Shit.

(faintly audible sobbing)

Audio File Transcript #4

Okay, I learned something new after getting into politics. There's this thing called "opposition research." It's where you dig in the dirt and find out the worst things you can discover about a person. Then you take that bad stuff and twist it to make it sound even worse. Then you bring in some semi-related stuff that seems like it might be true if you assumed the absolute worst about a person. Then you just make up whatever shit you want to because people will believe anything if you sell it hard enough.

Yeah, of course I did some stuff like that during my years in business. A little blackmail can help grease the skids when you need to get some shady shit done in a hurry. So I always knew about "opposition research." I just never knew that's what it was called.

But here's the thing I really learned: *Opposition research isn't the same thing as actual research.*

My advisers have told me all the opposition research about Hillary Clinton. It's the same shit we've been hearing for years. You know

... she's a bitch, she gave away secrets with her email, she killed people in Benghazi, her Foundation is a slush fund, she's a secret lesbian, she has her enemies murdered, blah, blah, blah.

Yeah, all of that is complete bullshit. Okay, one little part of it is kind of true. She had a private email server. So what? So did tons of big shits in the government at that time. But she's running for president, so she has to be crucified with opposition research, whether it's true or not.

Like I said, opposition research isn't the same thing as actual research. I went behind my dumbass advisers' backs the other day and asked one of those young interns to do some actual research about Hillary. This intern was a guy, by the way, so don't go getting any secret blowjob ideas. I picked a guy on purpose so I wouldn't be tempted to grab his pussy. Hey, maybe I'm evolving!

Anyway, I told this intern who is a guy and has no pussy to do it like he was writing a research paper for college. No spin. Just facts about her accomplishments, all objective like. Goddamn, I hated bullshit college.

But holy shit, this stuff about Hillary fucking floored me!

Hillary wasn't born with a silver spoon up her ass like I was. Bill was the same way. He was hillbilly poor, and she was Midwest middle-class. My dumbass supporters hate the fact that the Clintons have money now, but they don't seem to care that I shit on gold toilets in gold bathrooms and wipe my ass on stacks of thousand-dollar bills.

Those fucking Clintons worked for every fucking thing they ever got. Me? I mostly had everything handed to me by Daddy. Sure I had to kiss his ass for a while, and I had to follow him around and do a bunch of no-show, no-brain busy work for him. But he made sure I'd never have to work a real day in my life.

Of course, I knew Hillary did well in school. All of those fucking Democrats did well in school. That's one of the reasons I'm a Republican. It's the party for people who suck in school. But Hillary's like a certified goddamned brainiac! She was graduation speaker at her own fucking college graduation. Who does that shit?

Then she went to law school and did even better in class than Bill did. And she didn't even have to do that well because she was a little fucking hottie back then. Not Miss Universe material, of course, but she had something going for her. I've never gone for the intellectual types because it's hard to keep it up when you feel stupid. But some of those pictures of her back then, whoa! They'd make pretty decent whacking material. Don't tell Melania I said that! She'd put out even less than she does already.

Anyway, after law school, she could have gotten a big-time Wall Street job, but she didn't. She studied children and wrote a big fucking report about children's legal rights. Fucking children! She could have been making millions, but she was writing about fucking children instead. You won't hear that on Fox News.

And then she was a fucking spy. No shit. A fucking spy. Not like in Russia or anything. She went undercover to help investigate racism in Alabama schools. While I was getting sued for housing discrimination for not renting to Blacks, she was risking her life pretending to be a young housewife with kids going into the white-sheet-type schools to show that they were racist. Those fuckers would have killed her and buried her under the school if they caught her. That took way more balls than I've got, that's for sure.

Then she worked for the goddamned Watergate Committee. She was working against government corruption when I was still following my dad around collecting rent. She was helping get rid of Tricky Dick Nixon. Makes me feel ashamed for calling her "Crooked Hillary." And shame is not an emotion I have much practice feeling.

She did all kinds of shit for women's rights when she was with Bill in Arkansas. Sure, you'd expect that women's lib stuff from a young liberal back then, but she also worked on all kinds of children's rights and educational things too. Real housewife stuff. Stuff that you'd expect some Rotarian wife to be doing.

When she was First Lady of the whole country, she ran the whole fucking health care reform stuff. There was "Hillarycare" before there was "Obamacare." If the asshole Republicans and some limp-dick Democrats had helped her out, we wouldn't be in the fucking mess we're in today. And she did help get health insurance for millions of kids. It's called "Chips." No, not the TV show.

By the way, speaking of health care, my advisers tell me I have to hate Obamacare because it has the word "Obama" in it, but to be honest, I don't even know what Obamacare does. Maybe I'll secretly get that intern to research it so I know what the fuck I'm talking about for a change.

Then she went to China and said, "Women's rights are human rights." China! Those fuckers hate women almost as bigly as I do. Jesus, I'd give my left nut to say something that profound just once in my life. I'm stuck with "You're fired." Lame! Sad!

In the Senate, she fought for health benefits for first responders and military veterans. I said in the debates that she should have changed all the laws when she was in the Senate, but the other day I saw a scholarly video about how laws get made, and I realized that I was talking out of my ass again, as usual. You should see this video. Very academic shit, okay. High-level shit. And a catchy tune.

(singing) "I'm just a bill. I'm just a bill. And I'm crapping here on top of this hill ..."

(back to normal speaking voice) Something like that.

All everybody wants to talk about from her time as Secretary of State is her email, but she managed to get the country out of the international shithouse that Bush flushed us into. She kept us out of a dozen big new wars that Romney or crazy Grandpa McCain would have started. People make fun of that Iran deal, but the fucking experts say it's the best chance to keep the Ayatollahs from becoming the world's biggest ass-a-holahs.

And, shit, she was in the room when we got Osama. In. The. Fucking. Room. I was still crying because Obama made fun of me the day before a the goddamned Nerd Prom corresponding dinner thing.

Yeah, if the people out there actually did the minimum bit of research that my intern did, they'd know that she's the best candidate, better than me by a few million miles. But they'd rather just listen to the propaganda. They're happy to believe every lie ever told about Hillary, and Obama for that matter, but they refuse to believe the truth about a rich, white asshole guy like me.

Like my buddy Don King always says, "Only in fucking America."

Audio File Transcript #5

It's not rocket surgery how we used that "opposition research" shit to get people to believe that Hillary was evil. Let me explain it to you because people seem too stupid to understand how we pulled off this particular long con.

Here's a clue: The people who know Hillary the best and have actually worked with her, they all love her and would follow her to hell and back. The fuckers who hate her and talk shit about her all day, guess what? Those bastards don't know anything about her, have never worked with her, and have probably never even been in the same fucking room with her in their whole miserable lives.

Here's how we were able to take the multiple most-admire woman in the world and make so many ignorant suckers hate her.

First, she's been attacked since before she was even First Lady. Bill did well for a fat hillbilly, but Republicans knew Hillary was the real star way back then. So they started criticizing her for not baking cookies and having an actual job. Most Republican men hated her right from the start just because she was smart and strong and didn't just flash her tits at everybody. It was easy to get them to see her as some kind of she-devil.

Republican women were a little harder to convince. But they're a repressed and self-hating bunch anyway. We got them to hate her because she stuck with Bill when he fucked around. That was a laugh because they would have hated her for being independent and dumping him, but they hated her just as much for being a good wife and sticking with him. No matter what the fuck she did, she couldn't please anyone ever, thanks to Republican attacks.

Hillary called it a "vast right-wing conspiracy," but even she didn't know how fucking bigly vast it was. They kept that shit going for decades, all the way through her first run for president. Then, when she ran this time, they knew she had a great chance to win, so they turned on the bullshit spigot like no one had ever seen before.

Fox Fake News and Drudge Sludge had been the head attack monkeys for years, but then that first-class asshole Andrew Breitbart took over. He turned fake news attacks into an art form. Then he drank himself to death or something because even he couldn't stand what a fucking asshole he turned into. That's when my buddy Steve Bannon took over. You know him. Fat guy. Needs a bath. Hates Jews. Smacked his wife around. My kind of guy. He got the major right-wing money machine involved, and even got the lazy corporate media to lap up his sour milk.

Breitbart is pure propaganda for the clueless deplorables, and lots of these Republican even follow true mental cases like Alex Jones. This numbnuts thinks that 9-11 was an inside job. He'll froth about "false flags" and claim that Obama and Hillary faked all those shootings at Aurora, Sandy Hook, Charleston, and Orlando to make people want tougher gun laws.

The fucker even thinks Obama faked the Boston Marathon bombing. I guess he's afraid of bomb control as much as he is of gun control. Pretty soon he'll be ranting that "the only thing that can stop a bad guy with a bomb is a good guy with a bomb." Goddamned bombs in every home! Fuck, I'd better check that sometimes because the asshole probably did say that.

Hell, the fucking gun nuts just buy more fucking guns, as if that'll make a difference.

They have their shoot-'em-up movie playing in their little minds. No need to blame the government. Fucking Alex Jones says Obama has a weather machine to control hurricanes and tornados. The guy's a fucking freak.

Guess what? I went on his show. I talked to his mind-fucked audience. I kissed up to the worst of the worst. And I did it just to make crazy people who already hate Hillary hate her even more. Like the fuckers think they get extra votes because they have extra hate and extra crazy.

Remember the bullshit stories about the Clinton Foundation handing out all kinds of favors to donors when she was Secretary of State? Not a single word of that shit was true, but the *New York Times* and *Washington Post* printed it like it came straight from liberal Jesus himself. That's fucking hilarious. These liberal rags were attacking Clinton just because they were jealous and lazy and stupid. So a foundation that helped millions of people suddenly became a slush fund for those evil Clintons. And the public swallowed every bullshit word of it.

Then the Ruskies got involved. Pootie-Poot and his rich oil buddies started hiring hackers to leak shit to Wikileaks, and those morons spread it all like jelly on burnt toast. I kept saying that it might not have been Russia that did the hacking, but that's just more bullshit to cover my ass. People on my staff have all kinds of ties to Russia and were even in touch with Russia during the campaign. It's not like that's a fucking secret. I keep saying it could be some 400-pound guy on a bed in New Jersey, but that's just my way of poking fun at that fat fuckwad Chris Christie. Of course it's the fucking Russians. Jesus, any idiot should know that.

All those hacked Podesta emails? That was a big-ass nothingburger that the dumbass media kept feeding people to satisfy their crazy Hillary hate. Seriously, that Podesta and DNC email shit wasn't even close to the shit that came up at every campaign meeting in the history of forever. Republican said shit a thousand times worse, but Putin kept that shit in the toilet instead of dumping it all over the floor. If I accidentally win this thing, Putin will send out Christmas cards with him shirtless horseback riding me. I'd be his bitch for the next four years.

Vladdy also got lots of Russian slackers to start spreading fake news all over the internet for fun and profit. Lots of

Republican operatives were doing the same thing here, which everyone knows about but pretends not to. These fakers posted the most ridiculous crap you can imagine, and people fucking believed it. According to these hucksters, a secret code in the Podesta emails showed that Hillary was running a child sex-slave ring out of the basement of a pizza joint that didn't even have a basement. And the fucking morons believed that shit!

They believed that a seventy-year-old grandmother who has been a child advocate all of her adult life and wrote a book about raising children was actually running a child sex-slave operation. And I'm the one who actually has a lawsuit accusing me of raping a thirteen-year-old girl, but they claim that's just made-up crap. Did I rape a thirteen-year-old girl? I'm sure as hell not telling you fuckers. I don't want to be president, but I don't want to go to fucking jail even more.

Another fake news story is that Hillary murdered all the people who were going to prove that she won the nomination by stealing votes from Bernie Sanders. What bullshit! She beat his old, bald ass by millions of votes. Even Bernie said she won fair and square. I'm completely amazed that people will believe the most ridiculous lies about

Hillary, but they'll ignore the truth about all the illegal and unethical shit I've pulled over the years. Don't get me wrong. I'm glad people are that fucking stupid. But it still just amazes me how easy it is to scam them. When you're as famous as I am, you can scam 'em right in the pussy and get away with it.

Here's the funniest part. The fake news spammers tried to attack me and other Republicans with false stories, but the goddamned liberals and Democrats did the minimal amount of fact checking needed to prove it was all bullshit. Republicans flooded their Facebook pages and Twitter feeds with the biggest lies imaginable and called anybody who question them, "Kool-Aid Drinkers." Democrats didn't swallow the bullshit for a minute.

And then those Russian slackers would get fake social media profiles and jump into the comment section to troll everything they can find with the worst fucking grammar in history. Here's a fun game: Read some of those troll comments. Guess which ones are from Russians who don't know English and which ones are Trump University graduates who don't know English any better. Good fucking luck.

Of course, Republicans believe anything you tell them even when it's not even close to true, especially when I blamed Hillary for things that I was obviously guilty of myself. "Crooked Hillary?" Shit, is anybody more crooked than I am? Fuck no. When I call Hillary a liar? Who lies more than I do? Nobody. When I call Hillary, "nasty"? Jesus, has anybody been listening to me? Between pussy-grabbing and mocking disabled reporters and seeing a ten-year-old girl and saying that I'd be dating her in ten years, I'm the nastiest fucking piece of shit imaginable. But people blamed Hillary for all that shit instead of me. Are they fucking blind, deaf, and stupid?

All of this was only possible because Fox News has been setting the fake news table for two fucking decades. They're the mother of all fake news. Fake news has been sucking Fox News's titties longer than Putin has been murdering journalists he doesn't like. Republicans have heard so many lies for so long that they have no idea what planet they're living on. And I pretended that I was better than everybody by staging a fake feud with Fox News. Fucking Megyn Kelley bleeding from her whatever. What a bunch of bullshit. I fucking love Fox News!

Yeah, fucking Roger Ailes has been one of my closest advisers right from the start. He's my sexual harassment brother from another mother fucker, my comrade in pussy grabbing. Without him getting me on *Fox and Friends* to spread my bullshit for years, I wouldn't even have had a chance in this election.

But you know what's really deplorable? It's not that people can be fooled so easily by con artists. That kind of shit has been happening since the dawn of cave man time. What's deplorable, what's truly fucking pathetic is that people can be fooled by a con artist as shitty as me.

It's not like they're believing in Bigfoot, okay? Big fucking man-ape lives in the woods. It could happen, I guess. I can sort of understand believing in Bigfoot. That's about the same level of idiotic belief that it takes to believe that, oh, let's say, Chris Christie would make a good fucking president. It's dumb, but you can kind of see it if you squint really hard. It's not even like they're believing that Bigfoot would make a great president. It's more like they believe that a two-hundred-fifty-pound bag of Bigfoot shit would make a great president.

I'm a two-hundred-fifty-pound bag of Bigfoot shit, and these idiots want to vote for me to be president. And if someone tells them, "Excuse me, but I don't think a two-hundred-fifty-pound bag of Bigfoot shit would make a good president," these fuckers start screaming that they're a commie, pinko, America-hating, snowflake, ISIS-diddler who should die right fucking now.

I mean, think about it. I've spent my whole life doing nothing but getting money and then pissing it away, getting money, pissing it away. Getting. Pissing. Getting. Pissing. Like a big bag of Bigfoot shit.

That qualifies me to be an asshole, not president. I'm pretty fucking cynical, but I'm still having a hard time wrapping my head around the fact that millions of Americans have been eating the candy-coated Bigfoot turds I've been serving up my whole life. If I'm not careful, these morons might even get me elected to a job I wouldn't even wish on my worst enemy.

Fuckers. I hate 'em all so much that I wouldn't even grab any of 'em by the pussy.

Audio File Transcript #6

Note to self, asshole: *Stop drunk tweeting at the ass-crack of dawn every fucking day.*

The ass-crack of dawn every other fucking day is plenty.

My fucking Twitter feed is way more embarrassing than anything they hacked from the Hillary campaign's emails. But my Twitter shit is right there for people to see, and some of them are still going to vote for me. I keep trying to warn them that I'm an asshole, but they keep eating it up like candy.

If that tweet about Miss Universe's sex tape didn't send them running to Hillary, nothing will.

Jesus, what the fuck do I have to do to lose this fucking election!

(sound of objects breaking followed by heavy breathing)

Audio File Transcript #7

Okay, somebody help me with something that's been bugging me. What's up with those "Bernie or Bust" douchenozzles? I don't know whether to thank them or tell them to shut the fuck up. They love Bernie. I get that. But they think Bernie is a saint and Hillary is evil? Are they even fucking paying attention?

Here's a question for them: What's the difference between Bernie and Hillary on the issues? Bernie loves pot and guns and hates fracking a teeny, tiny bit more than Hillary. End of story. Even I know that, and I avoid thinking about the issues as much as I can because it makes my fucking head hurt. Otherwise, they're pretty much identical.

Yeah, sure, Bernie's a lovable old commie and Hillary's the school teacher the Bernie Bots hate almost as much as my supporters hate her, which makes no fucking sense. Fuck, twenty years ago, everybody thought Hillary was a big fucking liberal. Now the Bernie Bots think she's a secret Republican. Seriously? What the fuck?

Yeah, Hillary took money from Wall Street and Bernie didn't. So fucking what? Do these moon children even know that *I am fucking Wall Street?* They're worried that Hillary gave speeches to Goldman Sucks? Jesus and every goddamned disciple, don't they know that I'll put fucking gold men from Goldman on my cabinet if they're dumb enough to elect me? Some days it's hard to keep up the act when the suckers suck so hard. There's no challenge in it when people are dumb enough to think Hillary is as fucking awful as I am.

Hillary's biggest mistake in this campaign is that she treated voters like they were good, smart people. She ran as if people were looking for someone to do good things and help people. She talked in complete sentences about complicated shit. The only reason Bernie beat her in some primaries is that he knew people were dumb and mean. He channeled their cave man stupidity and anger at Wall Street. "Wall Street bad! Hillary love Wall Street! Me hate Hillary! Me crush Wall Street! Me vote Bernie!" What a barn full of horseshit.

Hillary gave speeches to Wall Street to make money. Big fucking deal. My staff got hold of those precious Wall Street speech transcripts everybody was screaming about, and almost all of it is do-gooder shit about helping people and hiring women, blah, blah, blah. She said a few things about how Wall Street can be part of doing good things by helping people get the funding they need for buying homes and running businesses, yada, yada, yada. She didn't release the transcripts because she knew that, no matter what was actually in her fucking speeches, the fucking Bernie Bot cavemen would grab their clubs and yell, "Smash! Smash! Smash!"

Hillary said that Wall Street should actually exist but just be heavily regulated to keep the crooks minimally honest. That takes more than a caveman brain to understand, so that sent a lot of voters over to an old Socialist who isn't even a real Democrat and never had a real job in his life. Bernie is even campaigning for Hillary now, but those cavemen bots might not vote for her, and I might accidentally win. Jesus, I hope not. I'll strangle Bernie myself if that happens.

Between me and Hillary, one of us is fucking awful, that's for sure. One of us has a long history of idiotic and illegal business practices. One of us is a rude mother fucker. One of us has semi-subtle racist views. One of us has clearly misogynist tendencies. One of us knows next to nothing about the issues. One of us has no government experience. One of us lies constantly and then claims the system is rigged whenever those lies are called out.

The other is Hillary Clinton.

Are they going to vote for Jill Stein? Like she has a fucking chance. They're too fucking young to remember Ralph Nader. Go ahead and vote your conscience and see what happens. I could squeak by in a few states and actually win the fucking Electoral College while Hillary wins California by a billion votes and wins the overall popular vote. That's pretty much how we got Jebbie's brother. Yeah, laugh about that, Bernie or Busters! It's the only fucking way I could win, and nobody actually wants me to win, least of all me!

Yeah, Bernie gets rallies. Big fucking rallies. Big fucking deal. I get rallies too. Bigly. I have the biggest rallies, okay? But my rallies are filled with old, crazy fuckers. Bernie's are young, idealistic fuckers. The difference is that old, crazy fuckers show up and vote. Young, idealistic fuckers talk a big game but sit on their asses rolling doobies and playing video games on election day.

You know why there's no "Hillary or Bust" movement? Because Hillary supporters are fucking smart enough to know that "bust" is me. If they hold out for their perfect candidate instead of settling a little bit for one that's almost as good, then they're going to put me in office. And I sure as hell don't really want to be president. You have to actually get shit done instead of just complaining about everybody else.

Come to think of it, that might be the biggest difference between Hillary and Bernie. She's gotten shit done for decades while Bernie has complained. Sure, the world needs complainers. I'm the best fucking complainer in the fucking world. But maybe the president should be someone who actually knows how to get shit done.

I might have had a chance to beat Bernie if the Dems had been confused enough to nominate him. Can they really not know that the Republican scumbags have a file two feet thick on all the shit we can pin on Bernie? I've seen that file. Sure, some of it is pure bullshit, but some is fucking true and fucking ugly. And when has pure bullshit ever stopped Republicans? If we had to tell the truth about Hillary, she'd be up fifty fucking points in the polls.

Lying is what Republicans do best. And lying about Hillary is the only fucking chance we ever had to win.

Audio File Transcript #8

Why did no one tell me that fucking Dr. Oz was a Muslim? I know he's a con artist, and that's fine. This pot ain't calling that kettle black for that reason. But a goddamned Muslim? I thought my supporters would throw a shit-fit when they saw me on TV with a Muslim.

Oh, wait a second. We're talking about *my supporters* here. They're too dumb to know that he's a Muslim. They probably think he's a wizard. And even if they did discover he's a Muslim, they'd probably just say some dumbass thing like, "Oh, he's one of the *good ones*. Not like Osama Osambo Hussein Obummer." Jesus, these people. I don't fucking ever want to fucking spend ten fucking minutes in the same fucking room with the fucking morons who would fucking vote for me.

Okay, while I'm on the subject of religion, somebody out there explain something to me. Why the fuck do evangelical Christians support me?

If I stood in their pulpits and talked about pussy grabbing or wanting to date my own daughter or bragging that I'm better than everyone else, would they nod their fat heads and mumble, "A-fucking-men"?

I guess when millions of people brag that their imaginary friend in the sky can beat up everybody else's imaginary friend in the sky, it's not hard to get them to believe the bullshit that a professional asshole like me gives a shit about them.

I never bothered to read the Bible, but even I know it says you should treat immigrants and refugees as if they're your own family. How would these Bible-thumpers like it if I called them and their families rapists and murderers and drug dealers? How would they like it if I said I was gong to ban their families from coming into this country?

They blather on and on about their sweet baby Jesus, but do they even know that Jesus was a Middle-Easterner? These morons would run from Jesus if he walked into their church. They'd call the police and have him shipped back to fucking Mexico. I doubt they can even tell the difference between a Mexican and a Middle-Easterner. Fuck, all of their churches have pictures of blond-haired, blue-eyed Jesus as if he were a

Hitler Youth Camp counselor. I'm the Aryan, not fucking Jesus.

Don't they know what Jesus said about rich people like me? I'm sure as shit not going to Jesus heaven when I die. Don't they know that Jesus would tell me to fuck off?

You know who actually loves Jesus? Fucking Grandma-on-Sunday Hillary and Choirboy Obama love Jesus. Democrats love Jesus. Bernie the Jew loves Jesus more than these idiotic Iowa Christian Republicans. Bernie wants to help poor people. Guess who else wanted to help poor people? I'll spell it for you: J-E-S-U-fucking-S. Barack Hussein Obama with his sandstorm name loves Jesus a fucking shitload more than I do.

Sure there are some Christians who aren't complete idiots. They help people and work for peace and spread love and try to make the bullshit world less of a pile of bullshit. Those fuckers vote for Democrats. If they ever took control of their churches, hucksters like me would have no chance.

I fucking hate Jesus. Isn't that obvious? Does anybody really believe that Jesus would talk about nuclear weapons like I do?

Shit, the seven deadly sins are like my daily events calendar: Pride, 7:00 a.m. Envy, 7:15. Wrath, 7:30. Gluttony, 7:45. Lust, 8:00. Greed, all fucking day long every day. The only deadly sin I don't have is sloth. I'm not fucking lazy. I work hard at all of those other deadly sins all fucking day long.

The great thing about Republican Christianity is that it's a get-out-of-jail-free card. I can fuck around on all my wives and grab pussies and say completely fucked up things all the time, but those Christians will say that God forgives me just because I ask him.

And here's the fucking hilarious part: *I don't even have to ask for forgiveness.*

These fuckheads just pretend I want their fucking forgiveness. In fact, I even said on television that I never ask God for forgiveness because I haven't done anything that needs forgiven. But these dipshits forgive me and vote for me and claim God wants me to be fucking president anyway. How goddamned pathetic is that?

As long as I pretend to hate the homos once in a while, these assholes love me. Sure, adultery is forbidden in their Bible, and being gay is way fucking down there on the list with eating shellfish and wearing polyester. But just claim that gays want special rights, and every Republican Christian in America will forget that I've spent decades making adultery the official sport of Trumpistan.

Sure, lots of these Republican Christians love to bow down before a big daddy authority figure. They love their made-up dictator in the clouds. I've been trying to fill that role, but I'm a piss-poor substitute. I talk bigly every chance I get, but I'm just a scared little playground bully.

You know who's actually strong? Fucking Hillary is. Did you see the way she dragged by wrinkled suit around the floor in those debates? You'd think if these Christians wanted a tough president, they'd see that Hillary is about a thousand times tougher than I am. I crybabied about a three-hour debate, but she testified for eleven hours without even breaking a sweat. She fucking campaigned with pneumonia at an age when she's eligible for Medicare, for fuck's sake! I had a fake foot boo-boo when I was twenty-two to get out of Viet Nam. She probably could have won Viet Nam by herself.

But, of course, these fake tough Republican fake Christians couldn't stand for a girl as president. Their little peckers would shrivel up. Especially the Republican women.

As long as I keep humping about abortion, the Republican Christian numbnuts will love me. Those assholes don't even know that abortion isn't even in their fancy Bible. They don't even know that politicians have been lying about abortion for decades. Easiest thing in the world is to get a Republican Christian to ignore everything else you say and do. Just agree with them that abortion is evil. Just yell "baby killer" a couple of times, and they'll vote for you even if you plan to take away their health insurance ... which I plan to take away, in case anyone isn't paying attention. Maybe Jesus healed people, but I'm definitely not fucking Jesus.

And the gays. Just tell 'em I'll get rid of gay marriage, and they'll blow me they'll be so happy. Fucking Republican Christians think and talk about gay sex more than any gay people I know.

These fools keep asking me to pray with them. They keep wanting to hold my hand and touch me while they pray. I just bow my head and fake my way through it, but the whole thing makes me want to vomit. Not enough fucking hand-sanitizer in the fucking world for that shit.

Shit, can anyone imagine me praying? Here's my fucking prayer: "Thank God I was born wealthy, white, male, American, and straight." Without even one of those gifts, my real estate career wouldn't have advanced beyond gossipy overnight desk clerk at an hourly-rate motel on the wrong fucking side of the tracks.

What Christian hymns would I sing? "How Great Trump Art," "Nearer My Trump to Thee," and "O Come Let Us Adore Trump" aren't real hymns, but I sure as hell like the sound of them. If I actually had a chance to win this fucking election, I might try to use them for my imaginary inauguration because I'd have to blackmail any real celebrities to perform.

What would my sermons be like? Remember when I spoke at that freaky Liberty University? I said "Two Corinthians," which every dumbass Christian child knows is pronounced, "Second Corinthians." But I said "Two Corinthians," like I was starting a bad joke: "Two Corinthians walk into a bar ..." And they're still fucking stupid enough to vote for me.

Yeah, the goddamned joke's on the whole country, assholes.

Audio File Transcript #9

Goddamned *Saturday Night Live*. That shit really hurts my feelings because it's so goddamned true. Goddamned Alec Baldwin. Can I sue him? My lawyers say I can't because "satire is protected by the First Amendment, blah, blah, blah," and all that other legal mumbo jumbo shit. Constitution sucks. But I'd love to sue his ass for a bajillion dollars. Why can't that fucker be more like his brother Stephen? Sure, Alec is a million times more talented and famous and rich, but Stephen is maybe my third most famous supporter behind Jon Voight and that Chachi motherfucker.

You don't see Hillary tweeting about *Saturday Night Live* making fun of her. Hell, they've been making fun of presidents and politicians since that fucking stumble-bum Jerry Ford. Ronnie Raygun never jumped on *Saturday Night Live* when they made him look like a clueless old fucker. I know I shouldn't get mad at them and send those dumbass tweets at all hours of the night. But I'm just so fucking humiliated at how fucking good Baldwin's impression is. Fucker.

If I had any sense, I'd tweet some thing like, "Funny stuff from SNL. I hope they keep making fun of me when I'm president working to make the lives of all Americans better." Sounds like something fucking Obama would do. Classy mother fucker.

But that would be a triple fucking lie, of course. First, I want them *to stop making fucking fun of me!* Second, I don't give a shit about *making anyone's life better but my own!* And third, I don't *ever want to be fucking president!* I just want to blame everybody else and listen to the suckers cheer me at rallies like I'm Jesus Obama Christ.

Fuck, the president actually has to do something while assholes like me criticize him no matter what he does. That's the last fucking thing I want. If I actually win this fucking election, I'd have to hire a hitman to put me out of my misery. Blame that shit on Killary or ISIS or Bernie or Alec Baldwin.

If I win this fucking election, I'd have to be fucking *accountable*. I've never had to be accountable for anything in my life. I can fuck up anything I want to, declare bankruptcy, and then just use my famous name to get whatever credit I need.

Shit, even better, I can just sell my name whenever I want to. Think about all that shit out there with my name on it. People think I actually own that shit. Of course I don't, you morons. Other people own that shit, but they pay me to put my fucking name on it because morons all over the world think my name means something.

Shit, I could sell my name to a shit company, and they could call that shit, "Trump Shit," and the morons would buy it and talk about how it's the classiest shit out there and the best shit anyone ever shat. "Trump Shit is the huuuugest shit in the world! Only the bestest people buy Trump Shit! Buy Trump Shit and you can be as classy as Trump himself!"

What a bunch of shit! You people are buying shit and you don't even know it's shit! You shit heads voting for me are voting for shit! Shit, shit, shit, shit! Jesus fucking shit!

(long pause, audible heavy breathing)

If I win the election, I'll do a shitty job as president, and people will stop buying my fucking shit. I'll have to be accountable for the shit I do for the first time in my fucking life. I don't want that shit.

Nobody wants that fucking shit.

Audio File Transcript #10

Damn, it's fucking cold out today. It's as cold as a rally of my supporters ... zero degrees! Get it? Zero fucking degrees? Fuck, I love the uneducated! Shit that's a good one.

I'd laugh, but I realized recently that I never actually laugh. Has anyone ever seen a video of me laughing? Fuck no. Hillary laughs. Obama laughs. Bernie laughs about twice a year. Even that cross-dressing crypt keeper Rudy Giuliani laughs with his rotten chiclets teeth. Not me.

I smile now and then. Well, to be accurate, I smirk. Shit, search the internet thingy for, "Trump smirk," and you'll find fucking hundreds of pictures of my big face twisted into things that resemble a human smile if all the humanity were drained out of it. Fucking NBC uses one of those pictures that give me ten chins and more jowls than fucking Nixon.

But laughing? Not a fucking chance. You're more likely to find a video of me paying prostitutes to pee on each other than to find a video of me doing the simple, joyful human activity of laughing. I try sometimes, but I just sound like a fucking alien doing a bad human laugh impression.

Jesus, I never really noticed that until now. What kind of human fucking being doesn't laugh?

Audio File Transcript #11

Fucking Romney. Fucking Willard Ratshit Mittshit Dipstick Mother Fucking Romneyfuck.

I can't believe I endorsed that wax figure and campaigned for him in 2012. And he has the nerve to call me a fraud now? Fucking shitbird mother fucker.

Romney's a goddamned fucking fake-ass rich guy. Fucking squeaky clean Mormon. This guy would have a freak-out acid trip if he drank a cup of coffee. The guy never did a real day's work in his life, but he claims I'm a greedy bastard. I build shit. Okay, at least I pretend to build shit. Romney got rich tearing shit down.

I almost wish I could win this election just so I could humiliate this fuckwad. I'd pretend he was up for some cabinet post and have him grovel to me at Trump Tower. I'd take his pansy ass out to dinner and make sure the press got some pictures of him looking abso-fucking-lutely miserable. I'd cock-tease him for weeks and make it look like he was on the edge of getting a job.

I'd make him eat frog legs. Yeah, fucking frog legs. Fuuuuuuuuuuck him.

Then I'd fuck him over two or three more times and then pick someone even less qualified than him for whatever fucking secretary of whatever the fuck.

Fuck that good-haired fucker.

Audio File Transcript #12

It's no fucking wonder I got the Republican nomination when you consider the assholes I was running against. And how about the hardcore assholes voting in the Republican primaries? Jesus, what a bunch of knuckle-draggers. The voters *and* the candidates.

I just found a list of the people I ran against. Could barely remember half of those fuckers. I wouldn't even hire these guys to drive my fucking limo.

John Kasnich is so boring only cabbage and cow capital Ohio could elect him. He used to have a show on Fox News. Have they actually looked at his face? One word: radio.

Sped Cruz is a Canadian-Cuban who talks like a Martian. Yeah, I implied that his wife is ugly, but Ted's the one whose face looks like he's got a clown mask under his real skin.

Snarko Rubio makes my daughters look manly. At every debate, I looked around the audience to see if someone was operating him with a remote control. The guy's a fucking robot fairy or a fairy robot.

Charlie Fiorina has had at least as many fucking facelifts as I've had hair weaves that didn't work. Jesus, she may have fired even more people than I did. I know Republicans don't like to look shit up, but check out the way she lies about working her way up from the secretarial pool. Fuck, she's about as much of a fucking "self-made man" as I am.

Uncle Ben Carson could put amphetamine addicts to sleep. He's a brain surgeon who brags about stabbing his friends when he was young. Maybe it was scalpel practice for giving himself a fucking lobotomy.

Jeb Blush said his brother kept us safe. He must have been talking about Marvin, because that sure as shit wasn't what George did. And by the way, what the fuck is a "Jeb?" It's like a hillbilly mated with a snob. Your fucking name is "John," you pretentious mass of dough!

Chris Twistie endorsed me so that I could get 100% of the fat angry white guy vote instead of just 99%. That fat fucker left his fat fucking fingerprints all over that bridge bullshit. As soon as this election is over, he's getting dropped right off the side of that bridge. He thinks he's going to be Attorney General if I win. Shit, he's going to need an army of his own defense attorneys before this shit is all over.

Rick Sanitorium loves Jesus almost as much as I love myself. Damn, that guy's creepy. I'd think he was a closet case except that no gay guys I've ever met are that fucking creepy.

Mike Hucksterbee has turned Jesus into a profit center, which I actually kind of fucking admire. He should just name his TV show, "Jesus Said you Should Send me Money, You Dumb Fuckers!"

Take off the glasses, Prick Perry. You're still Texas-level stupid. Maybe I'll put you in charge of whatever department you couldn't fucking remember.

Lindsey Graham Cracker and Blobby Jindal look like they want to be in a tickle-fight with each other.

Snott Walker is a lazy-eyed, Wisconsin cheese-dick, college dropout motherfucker.

Randy Paul is even crazier than his fucking crazy-ass dad.

George Puketaki is really fucking tall, not that anybody cares.

Who the fuck is Jim Gilmore?

Basically, Republican politicians are so terrible that being terrible has become the main part of fucking their strategy. They figure if they're as terrible as possible, then everybody will be fed up with politics and blame both Democrats and Republicans, even though Democrats are actually trying to make things better for the whole country. Democrats aren't perfect, but, fuck, at least they try.

Republicans are fucking up on purpose and trying to spread the blame to everybody, especially Democrats. And it works. They control the House, Senate, and most of the states. Don't like the way the country is going? Don't blame the Republicans who have fucked up everything they've ever touched. Blame fucking Obama, the mild-mannered insurance agent who just wants you not to die because the insurance companies are trying to profit off of massive fucking piles of corpses. Or blame Hillary because she once used private email and has a weird laugh. Yeah, that shit makes sense. But it works for fucking Republicans and their dumbass voters.

My strategy was to be the biggest fuck up of all, basically be the worst politician of all time. It worked a hell of a lot better than I thought it would. Holy fuck, how it worked. Too fucking well.

And how about the so-called "independent" fuckers running for president? Who the fuck are they?

Gary Johnson? Too bad his first name isn't "Dick" and his middle name "Peter." You know, it's okay to be in favor of pot legalization. Who gives a shit? But it's not okay to give every TV interview acting like you're high as a fucking kite. I just hope nobody asks me about Aleppo. I have no fucking idea what that is, and my advisers have explained it to me a hundred times.

And "doctor" Jill Steinem? Never heard of her. Medical school must be easier than I thought. But, Jesus, she may just suck enough votes away from Hillary in a few states that I might manage to win the Electrical University shit. That would be just about the end of the fucking world.

Fuck 'em all. Ah, shit. Who am I kidding? Any goddamned one of 'em would make a less embarrassing president than me.

Audio File Transcript #13

People keep saying that I used to be a Democrat. I don't even know if that's fucking true or not. I ran for president in the Reform Party in 2000. Remember that? What the fuck is the Reform Party? Doesn't matter. I got my ass kicked.

I've flip-flopped so many times on so many issues over the years that I could be a pancake. Get it? You flip pancakes? I've seen it on TV. Never actually made food myself. Jesus, what a dumbass joke. Nobody will laugh at that except the fucking idiots who think I'll make a fucking good president. I can insult myself and they wouldn't even get the joke. Why are these fuckers even allowed to fucking vote?

My supporters think Democrats are evil. They're dumb enough to think I'm somehow better than the average Democrat. What morons. I'm worse that the worst Democrat on this planet. On any fucking planet.

Which Democrat said he gets his foreign policy knowledge from TV shows? I fucking said that. Out loud. I even said it on national

TV, but my supporters still think I have a fucking clue what I'm talking about.

Which Democrat's approach to the Middle East is, "bomb 'em and take their oil"? Which Democrat said he has a secret plan to destroy ISIS but will only reveal it if he gets elected? What kind of gullible hillbilly believes I have a secret plan to destroy ISIS? ISIS actually scares the piss out of me. I'll feel a lot safer when Hillary is dealing with those fucking monsters.

Which Democrat's biggest qualification for office is being a goddamned reality TV celebrity? Which Democrat kicked off his campaign by calling millions of people "rapists"? Which Democrat's campaign slogan is anything close to as dumb as, "Make America Great Again," as if America isn't already fucking great? Who the fuck came up with that dumbass slogan, anyway? He's fucking fired.

If Obama wore a baseball cap with my slogan, Republicans would make "America's Already Great! Go Back to Kenya!" their convention theme.

Which Democrat defends decades of nasty comments about women by claiming that it's okay because he only meant Rosie

O'Donnell? How does that make anything okay? Why the fuck do I act like Rosie O'Donnell isn't a real human being with real fucking feelings?

Which Democrat fake feuded with Megyn Kelly by talking about her bleeding from "wherever" and retweeting comments calling her a "bimbo"? Which Democrat makes comments about wanting to date his own daughter? Jesus, I'm a sick fucker. Which Democrat has a long history of calling anyone he disagrees with "stupid" and "a loser"? What's it going to take for my supporters to understand that I call people names because I'm a fucking asshole who shouldn't be allowed near the White House unless I buy a fucking ticket for a fucking tour?

Which Democrat proposed something as goddamned cruel and impossible as deporting millions of people? Which Democrat inspired two jerks in Boston to beat up a Latino homeless man and then claim, "Trump was right. All these illegals need to be deported."? I thought that one would hurt me in the polls, but the fake-liberal media didn't even touch it. How can this shit hurt me when nobody fucking knows about it?

Which Democrat said, "I will win the Latino vote" while polling barely double-digit approval among Latinos? I could wave a campaign sign that says, "Mexican Rapists for Trump," and my idiot supporters would believe it was real and cheer their empty fucking heads off.

Okay, once and for all, who is the Democrat's Donald J. Trump? What Democrat is as fucking horrible as me? Answer: No one. Not a fucking one.

Why? There's no fucking Democrat like me because Democrats aren't professional assholes. Republicans have cornered the market on professional assholes.

When I got into this race, I thought I'd probably poll at 5% and then drop out and declare myself the winner because I made people pay attention to me. Here's the thing: That's what would have fucking happened if I tried to run as a Democrat. Democrats are sane. Republicans are off the chart stupid and crazy.

I underestimated the asshole factor of the Republican Party. I couldn't have guessed that they would be deluded, ignorant, and nasty enough to see me as their fucking savior. Sure, I suck. But I'm just the stinking head of the Republican Party fish that's rotten all the way to the fucking tail.

Audio File Transcript #14

(Monotone generic voice, not Trump) I am grateful for your help. *YA blagodaren za vashu pomoshch'.*

(Trump, in thick fake Russian accent) I am grateful for your help, Vladimir.

(Monotone generic voice, not Trump) I am grateful for your help. *YA blagodaren za vashu pomoshch'.*

(Trump, in thick fake Russian accent) I am grateful for your help, Vladimir.

(Trump, in his normal voice) Fuck, yeah! He's going to be so proud of me he'll piss himself!

Hey, I didn't mean to turn this thing on. Shit. Stupid fucking assho--

(recording cut off in mid sentence)

Audio File Transcript #15

Okay, let's talk taxes. I claimed that I hadn't released my tax returns because I was under audit. Any idiot knows that's no reason to hide my tax returns. I hid them because they showed what a terrible businessman I am, fucking obviously. I lost almost a billion fucking dollars years ago, just like the goddamned *Jew York Times* says I did. Yeah, I said *"Jew" York Times.* This fucking election is almost over, so I don't give a shit what I say. Besides, am I wrong? They're all a bunch of Jews running that fake-news rag. Fuck 'em.

Anyway, who in their right mind would vote for me after finding out I lost almost a billion dollars? I'm shocked I didn't drop fifty points in the polls when that came out. But no, my fucked-up supporters just keep chanting about the fucking wall and the fucking swamp and locking up "Crooked Hillary." They aren't the deep thinking types, if you know what I mean.

And that's not all my tax returns would show. They'd show I haven't paid shit in taxes for years. What self-respecting taxpayer would vote for a fucking freeloader like me? Some asshole who makes $45,000 a year working like a dog isn't going to vote for me sitting on my fucking throne in my fucking castle and not giving a dime to the country. They'd have to be insane to vote for me if they knew how much I was screwing their asses.

Fuck, my tax returns would blow the lid off my fake foundation. I rag on Hillary about her foundation, but it gets great ratings from actual charity watchdogs. She actually helps people, millions of goddamned people. Fucking AIDS people. My foundation is a fucking scam. I paid my goddamned legal bills with money from my foundation. Hell, I bribed people with my foundation money. Republican Attorney General type people in states that were thinking of suing me for my Trump University con job. Does anybody even care that I got fined by the fucking IRS for doing that shit and then lying about it?

Republicans love their bribes almost as much as they love screwing people out of fucking health insurance. I screw people over for money, but these assholes do it just for the goddamned fun of it. Jesus, I can't keep all my scams straight between my unifuckistry and fuckdation. If anybody ever found out all the con jobs I've pulled with those fuckers,

I'd be sharing a cell with Bernie Madoff. Wait, is he dead yet? Who the fuck knows?

You know why I shit all over the press every chance I get? First, because the hillbillies who can barely read but vote every time love it. The press is full of smart people, and my supporters hate anyone smarter than they are.

(long pause)

So do I.

Fuck. Where was I?

Oh, yeah, the press. I shit on them because I know that if they ever touched my real tax returns, they'd see that I'm breaking about a thousand fucking laws. Hell, even the worst reporter on the planet would find deals with Cuba and Putin and a shitload of dictators in about five minutes if they had access to my tax returns. Even someone as dumb as Sean Hannity could find that shit. Good thing for me Hannity is about a mile up my ass right now. He's dumb as fuck, but he's like a dog with a bone if he gets his yellow teeth into your ass.

Those tax returns would also show that I've been lying about giving to charity, especially veterans' charities. Shit, just in this campaign, I claimed I raised six million dollars for vets, but I didn't give them a fucking dime. When the goddamned press started sniffing around that one, I eventually had to break down and give some veterans group a million. Fuck! I hate giving away money that doesn't come back to myself!

I used to think that saying I gave to veterans made me sound like a great fucking American, but the truth is that I never really liked veterans with their high-and-mighty attitude. They think their shit smells like strawberries and they want to rub everyone's faces in that shit. Hey, just because I never went to fucking war doesn't mean I'm any less of a man than they are. And don't get me started on women soldiers. Like I said before, you put men and women together in the military and you get rape. What the fuck do people expect?

I could've been a great soldier, you know. I could've shot my gun, *pew, pew, pew, bang, bang, bang,* and been a big fucking hero. I actually hate guns and think they're loud, germy, and a waste of time. But all I have to do is say that Hillary plans to repeal the Second Amendment, and the gun nuts think I'm Jesus fucking Christ packing an assault rifle. I even said something about "Second Amendment people" taking care of Hillary. Jesus, what an asshole thing to do, flirting with assassination. Thousands of my idiot supporters are about two fucking seconds away from shooting Hillary already without me opening my big fucking mouth. I'm turning the party of Lincoln into the party of John Wilkes Booth.

These pathetic gun boys love to show off their fucking boom-sticks as a way to compensate for their little peckers. Sure, I have a little pecker too. But I'm not stupid enough to use guns as my fucking overcompensater. I use women and money for that! Does anybody think I'd be able to grab all the fucking pussy I've grabbed in my lifetime if I didn't have so much money? Well, I don't really have that much money, but pretending to be rich is just as good when it comes to getting women to look past my ugly mug, hair weave, and puny pud.

Okay, so I had a foot boo-boo back in school, and I couldn't go to Vietnam. At least that's what my father told me. Big fucking deal. I didn't think my foot hurt that much, but my daddy told me to shut up and listen. He said he knew better. He was a fucking asshole.

I told Howard Stern that screwing women was like going to Vietnam. That was probably a dumbass thing to say. When I think about that, I can't imagine how anyone in the military would fucking support me. I said that going to a rich-kid military school gave me as much training as members of our armed forces. Born on third base and I brag that I hit a fucking triple. I actually said that, but my supporters didn't even fucking care.

I held a fundraiser for a fake veterans' group on a fucking battle ship. A fucking battleship! I actually did that. My numbnuts supporters didn't even notice. I said that our soldiers stole government money in Iraq. What the fuck was I thinking when I said that shit? Did my supporters care? Did they hold me accountable? No, those morons just kept wearing those stupid hats and yelling that Mexico would pay for the wall and Hillary should be locked up. What a bunch of fucking zombies.

I claimed that I had set up a hotline for veterans to call with problems, but that was a fucking sham. It just went straight to voicemail and told them to send me an email. That's fucking funny. If Hillary did that, CNN would talk shit about her 24 hours a day, and

Fox would call for her to be crucified naked live on their own network.

Okay, true confession time. Now that I've actually talked to some veterans on the campaign trail, I kind of feel bad that I've been screwing them over. Some of them seem like real heroes, not the fake kind like these retired generals who suck up to me. Sometimes it's hard to look these real veterans in the eye. They think I'm going to help them, just like they think I've actually given money to their charities. I prop them up at my rallies, but I just want to get the fuck away from most of them. They make me feel like an asshole because I called McCain a loser.

That one veteran gave me his Purple Heart. His Purple fucking Heart. And I fucking took it. I didn't know what to do because I felt so guilty that this poor sucker believed I was on his side. I took his medal and said I always wanted one. Jesus, I sounded like a fucking five-year-old. Somebody explained to me later that you only get a Purple Heart for getting wounded. Fuck if I want to get wounded. What kind of sick mind wants to get a Purple Heart without getting wounded?

(long pause)

McCain's just a grumpy old fucker. I'm the fucking loser.

Audio File Transcript #16

So, yeah, I suppose I should talk about that Access Hollywood tape. Shit. Yeah, that was me. It's not a fake. I really said all that stuff about trying to fuck married women and grabbing them by the pussy and all that shit. Am I proud of it? Fuck no. Even an asshole like me wouldn't be proud of that stuff being leaked.

Jesus, I make Bill Cosby look like Mr. Rogers. They're crucifying Bill Cosby right now. I know I'm not as likable as Bill Cosby. I'm not Mr. Jell-O Pudding Pop. But, hey, my clueless supporters have already let me get away with more shit than any politician in history, and they still show up at my rallies and join those robotic "lock her up" and "Mexico gonna pay for wall" chants. It helps that Cosby is chocolate pudding and I'm vanilla, if you know what I mean, wink, wink.

Yeah, I get away with it because he's fucking black and I'm fucking white, and white people can get away with all kinds of shit these days, in case anybody's too stupid to see that basic fact.

Did you hear me at the debate saying, "Nobody has more respect for women than I do"? Man, I almost gagged saying that mouthful of crap. Even I know that's the biggest load of bullshit since, well, since whatever I said five minutes before that.

Does the shit I said on that tape sound like I respect women? Yeah, me and that college swimmer rapist guy. We're real fucking Alan Alda types. I should have said, "Nobody tries to grab more pussy that I do." My staff probably wouldn't have like that. But forty-six percent of the idiotic American public would still vote for me anyway.

Is it the worst stuff I've ever said, that "pussy-grabbing" stuff? Fuck no! Thank Christ most of the other stuff I've said hasn't been leaked. I wake up every morning wondering what other shit is floating around from my toilet of a life out there. It's hard to look in the mirror and not wonder if today is the day that far worse stuff comes out or if today I'll get even worse blackmail threats than the ones I've already had to deal with.

I could claim that I was young and immature when I made those pussy-grabbing comments. That might have worked if I was a teenager or something. But, fuck, I was fifty-fucking-nine years old when I said that shit. You'd think I would have grown up by then, but no. Fuck no.

It's hard to believe people are shocked that I said all that shit. I guess they weren't listening when I said I wanted to date my own daughter. Ivanka, not Tiffany. Fuck no. Not Tiffany. Skank.

I guess they weren't paying attention when my leaked divorce papers said I raped Ivana because I was pissed off that she wasn't sympathetic when I complained about how much my botched hair transplant hurt. I guess people have forgotten when I bragged about all my affairs over the years. Shit, I cheated on my wives more that I cheated on tests in school, and cheating was the only way I could get through all those stupid classes. Well, cheating and being rich and not wanting to get the shit smacked out of me by my fucking dad.

My advisers want me to call the pussy-grabbing tape just, "locker room talk," as if that makes it fucking okay. They want me to say that it's all just talk and that I never did anything like that. Fuck, that's a crock of shit. They want me to say that Bill Clinton has done and said worse shit, as if people will be stupid enough to buy that excuse and blame Hillary instead of me. Can people really be that stupid?

"Locker room talk." Give me a fucking break. People are even saying that grabbing someone's crotch isn't sexual assault. Fucking Senator Jeff Sessions even said that it might not be sexual assault. Can you believe that asshole said that? Jesus, with that kind of blind loyalty, I should make him Attorney General if I'm unlucky enough to win this shit. Yeah, like anybody would let that racist turd be confirmed as Attorney fucking General.

Not sexual assault? Think about it. Picture it. I'm a big guy, six-two, way over two bills, closer to three hundred. Most women are a lot smaller than I am, you know, except their hands. I can't tell you how many times in my life I've marched right up to women, loomed over them, pressed myself way too close to them, tried to kiss 'em and grab 'em. I know it's wrong. Sometimes it even makes me feels sick to my stomach to realize that I'm that kind of person.

But I do it anyway because it's what I do. I get off on the power trip. I know I'm not the best looking guy around or the best personality or the smartest. Fuck, who am I kidding? I know I'm a homely, mean dope. And I haven't exactly gotten better looking with age. If I didn't have billions of pretend dollars, no woman would ever pay attention to me. So I do what I gotta do. I'm not proud of it, but it works to get me what I want, so I do it.

But "locker room talk"? What a bunch of bullshit. Let's try this. Whoever you are, even if you're a big, tough guy. Imagine someone bigger than you, more powerful, rich, famous, coming up close and looming over you, someone with powerful lawyers, the best lawyers, someone homely and mean and nasty, shoving his face down to try to kiss you on the mouth, wrapping an arm around you and yanking you against him, grabbing your crotch with his little hand, little hand that's still strong enough to squeeze your crotch in a way you don't ever want it squeezed.

Close your eyes and imagine that shit. Would you just call that "locker room talk"? Fuck no, you wouldn't.

And now the women are coming out of the woodwork. Women from decades ago are claiming that I harassed them, grabbed them, tried to fuck them. Shit, I'm not surprised. I knew this was coming, and I should have dropped out long before they started talking. What the fuck was I thinking? Just because I've been getting away with this shit for my whole life doesn't mean I can get away with it while running for a stupid fucking job that I don't even want.

The only thing that surprises me is that it's only about a dozen women who've come forward. All I can say is that the people arranging the payoffs did a pretty damned good job.

If there's any justice in the world, about a year from now, I'll be in jail. If I'm lucky, I'll be living in a trailer in West Bumfuck, Idaho, marching from one bumfuck house to the next bumfuck house, saying over and over, "Hi, my name is Donald J. Trump. I just moved into this neighborhood, and I'm required by law to tell you that I'm a convicted sex offender."

At least I won't be president. Can anyone imagine "President Pussy-Grabber"? Anyone who votes for me should have someone grab 'em in the fucking crotch and see how they like it. Grab 'em fucking hard.

(faintly audible sobbing)

Audio File Transcript #17

Jesus, Buddha, and Confucius, can you imagine if I actually win this fucking election? I'd have to read books like *Being President for Dummies* or *The Complete Idiot's Guide to Being President*. Oh, fuck it, who am I kidding? I don't read. I hate reading. Hell, I don't remember the last time I read an actual fucking book. I didn't even read the books that my ghostwriters wrote.

The suckers who read those pieces of fictional bullshit that have my name on the cover actually deserve someone as ridiculous as me for their president.

Obama writes actual fucking books. Hillary writes actual fucking books. I guess Hillary could be president of the people who read actual fucking books and have triple digit IQs, and I could be president of the Dumfuckistan deplorables. But who in their right mind would want that?

As if I'm in my right fucking mind.

Audio File Transcript #18

Why the holy-fuck-shit did I pick that goober-hillbilly Mike Pence for my VP? He doesn't believe in evolution or think that smoking causes cancer. Holy shit, does he live in a fucking cave?

Did you see those posters where it looked like the "T" in my name was fucking the "P" in his? Jesus Gaylord Christ. And when you put our names together into "trumpence," it sounds like the gayest sex act in Indiana. I can almost hear Pence now: "Yeah, baby, I want to trumpence all over your ass." Yuck!

Holy shit, the guy just left, and I practically had to tell him to get his pasty self out of here before I had Kellyanne drag him out by his limp wrists. Doesn't he have a bathroom to lurk in somewhere pretending to be policing cross dressers? Doesn't he have a fetus funeral to go to?

I thought picking the worst goddamned governor in the country was a safe bet against future impeachment, but I should have gone with fatso from Jersey instead. Fuck his lard-ass bridge bullshit. He might even be in prison before I am at this rate. I should have picked Giuliani or Gingrich. If you have to work with an asshole, might as well make it an old-school asshole. At least they have as many fucking divorces as I have. We could fucking commiserate about how much we hate the women we've fucked and fucked over.

Pence is a haircut masquerading as a man. The pansy keeps trying to hold my hand and pray with me and hug me. I think he kissed my fucking neck on the sly today. I've worked in the entertainment industry long enough to spot a closet case when I see one, and he's got more feather boas in his closet than Ru-fucking-Paul, who endorsed Hillary, by the way, the big sissy.

(audible knocking)

Oh, shit, the fucker is back. Get the fuck outta here you mother fuck--

(recording cut off in mid sentence)

Audio File Transcript #19

You know what no one ever says to me? "Prove it, asshole."

I could say the most fucking ridiculous thing, and no one ever says, "Prove it, asshole." Just once, I'd like someone to interrupt my lying rants about Mexican rapists or Obama's birth certificate or Hillary's crimes by saying, "Prove it, asshole."

What would I say back? I don't have any fucking proof for a single thing I ever say. People think I'm just "speaking my mind" or not bowing to "political correctness." Yeah, that's horseshit. I'm fucking lying.

People should know I'm lying. It's not a fucking mystery. Even I know that I'm lying. The thing is, everyone has let me get away with lying my whole life. That's one of the perks to people thinking I have money even though I've declared bankruptcy way more often than Hillary sent questionable emails. Imagine the lies I'd tell if I actually got elected president? What a fucking shitshow that would be.

But people just assume I'm telling the truth when, in fact, I'm lying just about every time I flap my fat mouth above my double fucking chins. And if people accuse me of lying, I just call 'em liars right back. Great strategy. Just take your own worst qualities and throw 'em back at your opponent. Did you watch the fucking debates? That was 90% of my strategy. "He said, she said," just like those groping accusations against me.

And just like the Nazis said, the bigger the lie, the more people will believe it. It's so easy to lie to Republicans anyway. Their party is based on more fucking lies than there are Grindr dates at the Republican National Convention.

Here's a big whopper: "Tax cuts for the rich will create jobs!" Bullshit. Tax cuts for the rich just make the rich richer.

Here's another: "Obamacare is Socialism!" Of course it's not. It's a private insurance program invented by Republicans to keep us off of single-payer healthcare, which is kind of actual socialism, sort of.

Want more? "Guns don't kill people. People kill people!" Jesus, that's the single dumbest thing I've ever heard. I pointed my fucking finger at my father a million times when I was a kid and went *"Pew! Pew! Pew! Bang! Bang! Bang!"* Guess what? The fucker never died. Why do you think that is? Maybe, just maybe ... because I didn't have a fucking gun, dumbass!

So, yeah, here's what I need and what Republicans in general need: Someone to say, "Prove it, asshole." It would be a relief to admit that I'm full of shit. Telling all the lies every fucking day is too much work. If I put half the effort over the years into learning the truth that I did in telling one lie after another, maybe I wouldn't have turned out to be the asshole that I am.

Shit, maybe I'd have turned out to be half the man that Hillary is.

Audio File Transcript #20

Fuck, I'm sorry. I'm sorry about this whole fucking shitty campaign. I thought I could win by being the biggest asshole on the planet. I'm fucking sorry that strategy got me even close to winning.

I'm sorry for claiming that Global Warming isn't real when almost every fucking scientists says it is. The high school dropouts in the Rust Belt think they're smarter than the science teacher who flunked 'em in ninth grade, so voting for me is their idea of revenge. What a bunch of fucking toothless morons. That's who's voting for me.

No wonder I'm losing this election. Who in their right mind would believe me when I said that the Chinese created global warming as a hoax? I mean, I blame the Chinese for a lot of things, but, most of the time, I have no idea what the fuck I'm talking about. The Chinese are just an easy group to blame because uneducated Republicans are scared to death of the Chinese. Is that bigotry? Sure, but when have I ever been above exploiting bigotry?

Global Warming is real, dickbrains. I'm the fucking hoax.

The Chinese are actually doing more to stop Global Warming than the U.S. is, but the folks who think they should vote for me don't know fuck about shit. Those fuckers think that Obama has a weather machine, and he's just trying to make them worship the devil. I'll probably carry the fucking snake-handlers voting block by eighty points. I might actually have a chance to win this election if they don't all die from getting bitten first. The snakes have better fucking teeth than they do.

Sure, people are pissed off. I can't blame 'em, considering how Republicans have been screwing 'em over for decades. I'm sorry for misusing the anger of everyday Americans to try to lie my way to the White House. I saw that anger and knew it should be directed toward wealthy assholes like me who put my greed above the good of our nation. I'm sorry that I tried to blame the problems people like me have caused for decades on people who've just been trying to help.

If I had any decency, I would have helped millions of Americans point their anger toward the wealthy and powerful who have squeezed the piss out of the American middle class. But I was one of those wealthy, powerful fuckers whose greed has chipped away at everything in this country. I've spent decades trying to make America into a few rich assholes like me at the top and millions of suckers doing my real work for shit wages at the bottom. I was one of the people who rigged the system against everybody else, but I lied and said that I was on the little guy's side and that I could unrig the rigging. I'm sorry I lied to everyone about all that shit.

I'm sorry I mocked a disabled reporter. Jesus, what's wrong with me? What's wrong with people who would laugh at that and vote for me anyway after seeing that? I'm sorry I enjoyed people laughing at me mocking him. I love to hear people laughing at someone else because that means they're not laughing at me. I'm sorry I lied and said I wasn't mocking him. I'm sorry that I'd rather lie than admit the truth to the public.

I'm sorry for the horrible campaign I've run during this election. Being able to avoid blurting out my worst thoughts, petty insults, and half-baked ideas is a good quality for a world leader. Hell, that's a good quality for a decent fucking human being. But that's not me.

I guess my shitty campaign shouldn't have been a surprise because I've been doing horrible shit for decades. Did I think no one would notice? I realize now that people can't be that dumb, can they?

I'm sorry for the way I attacked President Obama. You don't have to be Sigmund fucking Freud to understand that was because I was jealous of Obama. I was a little racist too, yeah, sure. If Obama's father had been from Scotland like my mother was, I never would have pimped this birther bullshit. But Scotland is lily-white, just like the deplorables who go nuts for the darkest Africa birther bullshit. So, sure, I was a little racist. Guilty. What can I say? I'm a Republican after all. But mostly, I was just fucking jealous.

I'm sorry I blamed Hillary for my birther bullshit. My advisers told me to say that. But even I figured out in two minutes of basic research that it isn't true. I guess my advisers figured my supporters are too lazy to do two minutes of research. Maybe I should blame her for all the pussy-grabbing too. My lazy supporters would probably nod

their heads and say they knew it all along.
Dumb fuckers.

I'm sorry for how idiotic my television show
is. I'm sorry for my ghost-written books that
make no sense. I'm sorry for bilking so many
people with my fake university and fake
foundation.

I'm sorry for all the underpaid people who
worked for me and all the contractors I
didn't pay. I'm sorry for getting away with
doing and saying so many obnoxious things
for so many years just because I was born
rich.

Shit, we all have at least one annoying, smug,
arrogant, confused, self-deluded, mean, lying,
pain-in-the-ass relative, right? We tolerate
that asshole at the holidays for the sake of
our family. Everybody puts up with the guy,
but nobody wants to get him elected
president. I'm that fucking asshole. I'm sorry
for being the fucking family asshole for the
whole fucking country.

I'm sorry for being a weakling who thought
that treating women like objects made me a
big man. I'm sorry for not realizing that
women are actual real people and not just
pussies to grab. I'm sorry for cheating on all

of my wives. What the fuck is wrong with me?

I'm sorry that I hired paid actors to cheer at my very first campaign announcement. You know, the one when I called Mexicans rapists. I'm sorry I called Mexicans rapists. What the fuck do I have against Mexicans? I don't even know any Mexicans.

I'm sorry for pretending to be smarter than our generals. What voters in their right mind would put me in charge of a real-life army? People die in a real-life army. I'd probably get real-life soldiers killed in some dumbass raid in my first week in office.

Just so everybody knows, this is not a fake apology like the one that my staff wrote for me after the tape of me bragging about pussy grabbing went public. This apology is real. I won't use this apology to blame other people. For once in my fucking life, I'm going to try to accept responsibility for what I've done.

I'm sorry I said that Hillary and Obama were the founders of ISIS. What kind of fuck head says asshole shit like that? I don't agree with everything Hillary and Obama do, but they're working hard and trying to make the world a better place. ISIS is a bunch of psycho murderers. They're the worst people on

Earth. Only a very sick mind would compare Hillary and Obama to ISIS. Jesus, I need so much professional fucking help.

I've acted like a terrible person as I've run for president. Am I a terrible person? I don't know. Probably. I've been so busy taking other people's money and blaming others and looking for the next person to attack and fantasizing about ruling the world that I've never really reflected on the meaning of my own fucking behavior.

I sure as hell seem like a terrible person when I watch myself in those three debates against Hillary. What kind of person shouts "Wrong!" when someone else is talking? A terrible person, that's who. If Hillary had said I interrupted her during the debates, I would have shouted "Wrong!" in the middle of her sentence. I'm sorry for debating like a toddler.

These idiot talking heads on the TV news claim that Hillary is too shrill and doesn't smile enough and seems too angry. What the fuck are they talking about? Don't they even watch me? I saw myself in those debates and wanted to punch myself in my fat, sniffling face. I'm sure millions of other Americans did too. Hell, compared to me, Hillary was as friendly as Mrs. Brady from the Brady Bunch. Thank God I'm not a woman. The way I shout and bark and grimace and interrupt, I'd be a fucking terrible first woman president.

I'm sorry I treated Hillary like she was a terrible person. I did everything but claim she was from Kenya. If I thought I could get away with that, I probably would have tried it. Some of my advisers suggested it, but I said that even my supporters aren't that dumb. But, fuck, maybe they are that dumb. Some of them believe that Hillary runs a sex-slave operation out of the basement of a pizza place in D.C. that doesn't even have a basement. That's one big-ass basket full of deplorables.

Two-thirds of my supporters think Obama is a Muslim. Even I know that's not true. More than half of these fuck-heads think he's a foreigner. Hell, almost half of them think Blacks are more violent and lazier than Whites. Shit, I used to think like that because I listened to my KKK dad too much. Did you know my dad was arrested at a Klan riot in New York City in 1927? The fucking press buried that little nugget. Can you imagine if Hillary's dad had been arrested at a KKK riot? No wonder the KKK endorsed me. My supporters would probably like me more if they knew about my KKK family connection. It would make them think of me kind of like a member of their family.

Here's a fun thing to do: Ask my supporters if they thought Lincoln made a mistake freeing the slaves. There was actually a poll about that. Go ahead. Ask 'em. You'll get a kick out of the results. Them's my people. Fuuuuuuck, I should be in jail for unleashing these shit-for-brains losers.

Have people actually ever listened to Hillary Clinton? She's way smarter than I am. She knows what she's doing. She actually has plans. Good fucking plans! The best fucking plans! I looked them up. Everybody should look them up. She makes sense. Smart people like Hillary have made me feel stupid for my whole life, but I'm beginning to realize that's *my* problem, not hers. I've obviously been bragging about how smart I am because I feel so fucking stupid inside. I hope it's not too late to change that pattern.

I'm sorry I never had plans. I'm all hot air. All I had were stupid walls and stupid slogans on stupid hats. Why does no one ask me what I mean by, "Make America Great Again"? When was America great if it isn't great now? The consultants who thought up that slogan never bothered to explain it to me. I'm sure it's supposed to mean that America was great before Obama ruined it, but that's horseshit.

Obama tripled the Dow and the S&P. He cut unemployment and the uninsured rate by more than half. He saved the auto industry and nearly doubled auto manufacturing. He cut the deficit by two-thirds and close to tripled consumer confidence. Gas prices are way down, renewable energy is way up, and our dependence on foreign oil is at a thirty-year low. I had to find all that shit on my own on the internet. My advisers never tell me that kind of stuff, and it sure as hell never gets mentioned on fucking *Fox-Fake-Fucking-News* or *Not-So-Fucking-Bright-Bart*.

Was America great when George double-spew Bush was president? We had the biggest terrorist attack in our history at the start of his term, an economic collapse at the end, and two mismanaged wars in the middle. I keep ranting that I opposed Bush's wars before they started, but everybody knows that's pure bullshit.

Was America great under Reagan? It seemed that way for rich assholes like me. But if you were working for a fucking living, the Reagan years sucked.

Was America great when gay people had to hide or get the fucking shit beat out of 'em? Was America great when it was legal for a husband to rape his wife? Was America great when women were basically not allowed to have a fucking job? Was America great when Japanese people were in concentration camps? Was America great when Blacks were getting lynched? How about when they were slaves? I'm sure some of my supporters think that shit made America great.

Was America great under Bill Clinton? Yeah, you know, it was pretty damned great. I'm sure Hillary will keep it great. Her slogan for reelection in four years should be, "Keep America Great." But she's too smart for slogans. She has plans instead.

I don't have real plans. Any fool can see that I just have crackpot schemes. I'm sorry for all those crackpot schemes. Let's all be thankful that I won't bring those schemes to the White House.

I need a fucking hobby. Or maybe I should replace this heart-shaped turd in my chest with the real thing. That would be a good fucking start.

Hillary is actually a good person. She's the opposite of a "nasty woman." I cringed when I watched myself say that at the debate on TV in front of everybody. It's like some evil fucking spirit possessed me. Hillary's not a criminal. She's a smart, hard-working person who cares way more about making America great than I ever did. Every time I called her "Crooked Hillary," I was just hoping that no one would notice what a crook I've been my whole fucking life.

Looking back on it, I can't believe how much I got off on hearing people cheer when I ranted about "Crooked Hillary." Jesus, these deplorables are so fucking easy to please. I used to get such a tiny, raging hard-on in my little micropenis when I heard people chant, "Lock her up!" I'm ashamed of myself for treating a good person like that, but I know I'm a pretty awful person when I'm being honest with myself. I don't like being honest with myself, in case anyone is too stupid to have noticed that quality about me.

I said that if Hillary were a man, she wouldn't get 5% of the vote. If I were a real man, I wouldn't feel the need to say such idiotic and sexist crap.

My Secret Service code name should be "Jellyfish" because a jellyfish's mouth also functions as its anus. When somebody asked me who I speak with about foreign affairs, I said that I had been "speaking with myself because I have a very good brain, and I've said a lot of things." Only someone with an asshole mouth would say shit that fucking stupid.

My advisers keep telling me that there's a chance I'll win, but I know that's just the yes-men bullshit I've been begging for my whole life. People only tell me what they think I want to hear. No one ever tells me the truth. The truth is that the polls tightened a little after Comey gave me that email horseshit on a silver platter. Giuliani told me that horseshit was coming. I'll bet Comey didn't even have grounds for a subpoena. I was shocked to see that the mainstream media ran with it, as if they couldn't tell the difference between Hillary's emails and Weiner's.

Jesus, I'm glad I never use email. Everybody keeps saying the mainstream media is in Hillary's pocket, so how come they spend so much time blathering about her fucking emails? I don't understand the whole thing, really. She used a private server. Big fucking deal. Her private server never got hacked, but the State Department server did. Even fucking Bernie said he was fed up with hearing about her fucking emails. Can somebody explain to me why my supporters have a shit-fit every time I put the words "Hillary" and "email" in the same sentence?

Shit, the RNC got hacked even though they keep pretending they didn't. Isn't it obvious to everybody what's going on? Russia is hacking the shit out of everybody, but they're only giving stuff that makes Hillary look bad to Wikipee, or whatever the fuck it's called.

Even the FBI keeps harping on Hillary's fucking emails. Comey said she didn't commit a crime, so you'd think that would be the end of the story. But then he farted on and on about her showing bad judgment. Then, after the whole thing falls into the short attentions span black hole, Comey sends a letter to Republicans and fucking CNN reads it on air and basically acts like the stenographer for the Hate Hillary Committee. Remind me to send Comey a fucking thank-you card. Or a hitman.

Shit, I hardly even need to run a campaign considering all the help I get from the media. Of course, my dipshit supporters hate the mainstream media, so I have to attack them. But, seriously, if goddamned Lindsey fucking Graham had gotten all the free coverage that I did, he'd be the fucking nominee instead of me. Can you imagine Senator Mint Julep as the nominee?

I did have my own email scandal once, but nobody cares, of course. A decade ago, a judge order me to turn over my emails when I was suing some nobody for nothing over some stupid casino deal. I made up some shit about our company not using email or routinely deleting it all or some such bullshit. Basically, I lied my ass off about my email, and nobody gave a shit. I got away with it because my name isn't "Hillary," and I've just got a little dick instead of her big balls.

Even with that little blip of nothing from Comey that the media went apeshit over, Hillary's still ahead in just about every poll. Sure, there could be some kind of fluke that lets me get enough votes from the deplorables while enough confused people don't vote because they're too dumb to see that I'm nowhere near as good a candidate as Hillary. It's possible a few states might flip if people get stupid, and the Electoral College might come into play.

I'm not really even sure what the Electoral College is. I never liked college. Is the Electoral College in Florida? That would be fucking great for spring break.

Can people really be fucking stupid enough to elect me? Jesus, I hope not. I don't want to be president now that I understand how much fucking work it is. I thought I could just be like a King and give speeches to adoring crowds and sign a few papers now and then with gold pens. Being president is actual fucking work. Obama works his skinny, black ass off, which drives the tighty-whitey-righties insane. Hillary will work her old lady ass off. But not my saggy ass. I don't want to do any *actual fucking work* involved in being president.

Fucking Putin works hard too, the crazy fucker. Everybody knows that meat-stick Putin hacked everybody's computers in this election to help me, but I hope he doesn't actually hack the fucking voting machines. I just heard that Pennsylvania and a bunch of other states don't have a fucking paper trail to validate the election. What the hell is wrong with them? Fuck, I might accidentally get elected if Putin hacks the voting machines. That would suck.

Hillary says that I'm a Putin puppet. Am I? How the hell should I know? I bragged about meeting Putin and then I lied and said I never met him. Or was I lying when I said I met him and telling the truth when I said I hadn't? I don't even know any more.

I'm like the world's greatest actress, Meryl Streep, in the *Sofa's Choice* movie: *(in a stilted accent)* "The truth, the truth? I don't know anymore what de truth is so many lies I have told." Pretty good Streep imitation, right? Yeah, not really. Fuck it.

Of course Putin wants me to win, but not because he thinks I'd make a better fucking president than Hillary. I've got so many business debts and ties to organized crime in Russia that Putin probably wants me in the White House to blackmail my ass. Shit, I wish business was all he had to blackmail me with. Did I work with Putin to influence this election? Duh. That's pretty fucking obvious.

Putin talks a good game, but he knows he's a worthless little piss without other people doing his dirty work for him. With all the shit he has on me, he'd make me drop Obama's sanctions faster than a Moscow hooker gets her job done in the winter. Then Putin could claim a great fucking victory against the powerful U.S. of A. Really, he'll just be able to make money again and do whatever the fuck he wants. Just like I'll be able to do after I lose this stupid fucking election.

Why does nobody notice that I talk shit about everybody else on earth except fucking Putin? The truth is that I have my nose so far up Putin's ass that Trump University will have to start issuing degrees in Siberian Proctology. If I do accidentally win this goddamned election, I'll have to threaten sanctions against the United States to keep us from investigating Putin's election meddling to try to help me win. Jesus, I need some fucking vodka.

Putin probably wants me in office because Hillary is one of the only people on the planet that scares that crazy Ruskie. She and Obama twisted his nuts so many times that he wants another Republican to just ignore him when he invades little countries.

Besides, if I actually did win, I'd go to bed every night scared shitless that the little monkey psychopath would climb in a White House window and strangle me in my sleep with piano wire. He fucking kills people who he doesn't like. Putin is old-school crazy, and nobody needs that particular recurring fucking nightmare.

Hillary will be a great president. You'll see. American already is great, and she'll help keep it great if you give her a chance and don't listen to ignorant blowhards like me.

The American president should be the leader of the free world. That's who Hillary is. I'd just be the leader of the fact-free world.

Hillary deserves to be president, and I deserve ... well, I don't even know what the fuck I deserve, but it ain't four years in the White House, that's for damned sure.

I'm going to go away and shut my big fat mouth for a long time. That's what America deserves after the crap I've just put this country through. It's like the old joke about the guy who wouldn't want to join a club that would have him as a member. I wouldn't want to be president of a country stupid enough to elect me president.

I'm sorry, Hillary. I'm sorry, Barack. I'm sorry Rosie. I'm sorry, everybody.

Now, where's the fucking taco truck? All this thinking for myself shit is hungry work.

Audio File Transcript #21

Okay, just a few more hours and I'll have to face the music. I forgot to tell anyone about these recordings, so my minions have been writing the speech on their own. Who cares what I say? I'm just a big fucking loser, and anyone with any sense knows it. I can't even fucking stand to listen to myself anymore.

It's a relief, really. They'll be coming to get me any minute now. I haven't been able to watch the news all evening because it's just too embarrassing. But it's for the best. We all know I would be the worst president ever.

(audible knocking)

Okay, okay, I'll be right there.

(muffled sounds as the recorder seems to be shoved into a jacket pocket)

(multiple muffled voices, unintelligible)

(Trump's voice, slightly muffled) What the fuck? Are you fucking kidding me? The Fucking Electoral Fucking College? Jesus Horatio Christ on toast!

(long pause)

Okay. Shit. Whatever. Jesus, people are fucking stupid. How the fuck did I win this thing? Only an idiot would want this fucking job.

I guess I'll have to be an even bigger fucking asshole than I was during the campaign to get people to understand what an absolute fucking asshole I am. The only bigger fucking assholes in this country are the fucking assholes that voted for me.

(long pause)

I don't know. Maybe this isn't as bad as I thought it would be. Maybe now people will finally like me. Maybe the smart people will finally think I'm smart instead of just the idiots thinking I'm smart. Maybe I am smart. Holy shit.

Son of a fucking bitch! I'm going to have the biggest, hugest, greatest, bestest fucking inauguration in history! Bigly!

(muffled sounds as the recorder seems to be taken out of the jacket pocket)

(Trump's voice, unmuffled again) Tiffany, get the fuck over here. Throw this goddamned thing away.

(muffled female voice, unintelligible)

I don't give a shit, you fucking dumbass! Just throw it away! Can you just do one goddamned thing right for a change? Fuck! Your brothers and sister are idiots, but at least they follow directions. What the fuck is wrong with you? I'm about to be President of the fucking United Shitty States of Trumperica! I own the fucking world now, and every last moron in this piece of shit country works for me now! So do what I fucking say for once in your worthless life. Dump this thing, you stupid bitch!

(door slamming)

(muffled sounds of recorder being dropped on the floor and then picked up)

(long pause)

(female voice) Fucking asshole.

(end of recordings)

Author's Afterword

On Tuesday, November 8, 2016, I worked from home most of the day, grading papers, planning classes, and writing. My monthly newspaper column for the *Daily Hampshire Gazette,* our hometown newspaper here in Northampton, Massachusetts, was due Thursday evening for Monday publication, so I set to drafting what I thought would be a reaction to Trump's election loss. I figured that he would end his run the same way he had campaigned: petty, dishonest, bitter, barely coherent, and with no sense of the damage his terrible presence in our national politics had created.

I wasn't overly worried or overly confident about the presidential election. Obviously, Hillary Clinton was a far better, more qualified candidate in every way. The majority of Americans would surely see that. But crazy things can happen.

And crazy things did happen.

In anticipation of Trump's "concession speech" being full of lies, bluster, and accusations of a "rigged election," my column included what I thought Trump should have said. I wrote an apology in his own voice as if he had finally realized that he owed the nation a massive apology--unfortunately, the apology we will never get from him.

That night, my wonderful wife Betsy and I watched the news coverage in horror as Trump remained competitive in Florida, Michigan, Wisconsin, and Pennsylvania. We couldn't believe that so many people could be confused, mean, and outright dumb enough to vote for Trump. We kept waiting for the urban centers, whose votes always came in last, to swing those key states for Hillary while California pulled her well over the top in the popular vote. As the dead of night descended, we fell into the dismal knowledge that Trump would hold on and eek out a thin Electoral College victory.

"Eek" was right, as in a horrified, "Eeeeeeek!" from the deep pit of my stomach.

I barely slept that night and had to face my community college students the next day. I had been telling those students that facts, research, critical thinking, civility, and empathy were keys to good scholarship and good citizenship. But the candidate who had violated each of those essential qualities had somehow won the presidential election. They were as depressed as I was.

For a brief time, I considered resigning my unpaid column-writing job. I thought I would have to discard my Trump concession column, considering Trump had won. I felt devoid of anything productive to say or write after such a shock. I considered never writing about politics and current events again. Instead, I could focus on fiction because nonfiction had just become so much less believable and so much less real.

But then I realized that we now live in an alternate reality. In the reality where we actually belong, Hillary Clinton is our president, and Donald Trump is just a bad memory and a worse Twitter account.

In this better world, much of my political activity would revolve around trying to get people to recognize the fact that Hillary Clinton's policies, like those of Barack Obama before her, were reasonable, progressive, and in keeping with the American values our nation has always cherished and nurtured.

Just as Obama had faced vicious and mindless hate, so too would Clinton in the better world where she was elected president. But I would keep plugging away at helping people see the truth. And, gradually, the Hillary-haters would be surpassed by people who recognized that she was the leader we needed to keep us moving forward.

In that better world, Trump had to deliver a concession speech. So I simply added a preface to my column indicating that this fictional speech was set in that better world, the real world where the unimaginable remained unimaginable.

In the face of Trump's victory, my column was well received and praised as an insightful look into the con artistry that had led to Trump's victory. The strong responses led me to start working on expanding the column into this book. I've never written so many swear words in my life, but I needed to capture Trump's infamous gutter mouth. I had to drink quite a few Angry Orchard Hard Ciders to deal with trying to write in Trump's profane voice. And I spent a lot of time scrubbing in hot showers just to feel cleansed after spending a few hours delving into his dark mind as I wrote.

Along the way, I made sure the book stuck close to that better world of facts and reality, even if I had to communicate those facts from Trump's twisted perspective. Pretty much everything in this book, despite its fictional format, is based on verifiable facts about Trump's actions, character, and campaign. The non-fact-based fictional elements I added here are the tiny portions of humility, humanity, and shame that I doubt he will ever actually feel.

All my life, I've written civil, scholarly, reasonable essays with some generous hints of satire. Trump's antics invite satire. Writing a book about him that is total satire wasn't that big a stretch, even if I had to stretch my writing enough to occupy Trump's big, wrinkled, lumpy, empty suit.

People have asked me if I'm afraid Trump will sue me. I'd rather he didn't, but we've all seen how he reacts to criticism of any kind. We should all aspire to a life that would prompt Donald Trump to sue us.

Satire is free speech protected by the First Amendment, but I'm glad that I personally know an ACLU lawyer. (Hi Bill!). Most likely, Trump will never hear of this book. Reading is not one of his strong suits. I'm sure I'll get some misspelled hate mail from the most deplorable of his supporters. But I already do get hate mail from them for my reasonable newspaper columns. Maybe I'll get one of

Trump's infamous hate tweets. A guy can dream.

Because we love our country, we have a job to do. Martin Luther King famously said, "The arc of the moral universe is long, but it bends toward justice." That arc got a lot longer on the dark night of November 8, 2016. That arc doesn't bend by itself. Our job has always been to keep it bending toward justice.

Our current job is to resist Trump's terrible and unjust policies and not be deflated by his embarrassingly awful character. Every day is the worst day of Trump's presidency, but we have to keep going in whatever way we can. Most days, I have no idea how to do that, but I keep trying. Most days, I cycle through the five stages of grief a dozen times in random order, but I keep trying.

We're all living these days in "Anyway world." I tell my wonderful wife Betsy most mornings, "Have a great day, *anyway*." And she does. And I do. And we try to make the days great for everyone else in whatever way we can.

The best advice I heard about how to go on during Trump's gloomy reign came from a singer I know. She said that we all have to keep doing what we do best. She needs to keep singing, as best she can, the songs that make the world a better place. She'll keep singing progressive, loving songs that combat Trump's regressive, cruel agenda. And she'll also sing songs that challenge Trump directly and open our nation's eyes to the ways that Trump violates the values that have actually made America great.

I'll keep teaching my students that critical thinking, evidence, creativity, and empathy are the keys to learning, growing, and being the best citizens they can be.

And I'll continue to exercise and eat mostly healthy foods so that I can outlive the Trump administration and see sanity restored to the White House. Maybe I'll even outlive Republican gerrymandering and see Congress come back to representative reality.

I'm a terrible singer, so I'll keep writing. That's one of the things I do best. I'll keep writing my civil, empathetic, and reasonable commentaries about politics and current events. And I'll keep writing gentle and not-so-gentle satire when people like Trump deserve it--which is often. Writing helps me have a great day "anyway" as I resist Trump and his enablers. I wrote this book to do my part for the resistance.

My grandchildren are one and three years old right now. Many years from now in better times, they'll ask me, "Grampy, what did you do to resist Trump?" And I'll be able to tell them, "I wrote a funny book to help people see how horrible Trump was, and the book also gave them a little hope and something to laugh about in a very sad period in history." And my sweet and smart grandkids will be proud of their old Grampy.

And America will be great again because we resisted Trump.

John Sheirer, March 2017

41444123R10083

Made in the USA
Middletown, DE
13 March 2017